Bill Crowdell

TRAFFORD

Printed in Victoria, BC, Canada

Note for Librarians: a cataloguing record for this book that
includes Dewey Decimal Classification and US Library of
Congress numbers is available from the Library and Archives
of Canada. The complete cataloguing record can be obtained
from their online database at:
www.collectionscanada.ca/amicus/index-e.html
ISBN 1-4120-2649-0

TRAFFORD

This book was published *on-demand* in cooperation with Trafford
Publishing. On-demand publishing is a unique process and service of
making a book available for retail sale to the public taking advantage
of on-demand manufacturing and Internet marketing. On-demand
publishing includes promotions, retail sales, manufacturing, order
fulfilment, accounting and collecting royalties on behalf of the author.

Offices in Canada, USA, UK, Ireland, and Spain
book sales for North America and international:
Trafford Publishing, 6E–2333 Government St.
Victoria, BC V8T 4P4 CANADA
phone 250 383 6864   toll-free 1 888 232 4444
fax 250 383 6804   email to orders@trafford.com
book sales in Europe:
Trafford Publishing (UK) Limited, 9 Park End Street, 2nd Floor
Oxford, UK Ox1 1HH UNITED KINGDOM
phone 44 (0)1865 722 113 (local rate 0845 230 9601)
facsimile 44 (0)1865 722 868; info.uk@trafford.com
order online at:
www.trafford.com/robots/04-0477.html

10   9   8   7   6   5

To

Carol

Simon and Oliver

CHAPTER 1

The door bell rang and Peter glanced at his watch - 11pm. A quick string of thoughts went through his mind 'Both sons are at home and Jane is playing badminton. Of course, she has forgotten her key'. He walked to the door, preoccupied as usual. The dark tall silhouette told him it was not Jane. The appearance of a Police Officer at 11pm cannot be good news.

'Mr Haynes?' said the policeman. 'Yes' replied Peter.

'May I come in?' They walked into the study in silence. Peter said 'It's Jane isn't it?'

'I am afraid so sir. She has been involved in a car crash'.

Peter asked the inevitable 'How bad?'

'Your wife has been taken to the Royal United Hospital, sir, in Bath. All I know is that she is unconscious'.

For the first time Peter noticed how young the policeman was. His genuine concern showed he was not yet hardened to 'the job'.

'I am sorry sir. I expect you will want to drive to the hospital straight away'. He turned away and spoke briefly by radio to his duty officer informing him that he had contacted the husband.

PC Enfield let himself out having ensured Peter had a car to get to the hospital.

Peter went to the playroom, as they still called it, and gave his sons the little information he had.

They were both young for their age and scarcely looked 13 and 15. He briefly told them the news and said 'I'm going to the hospital'. In unison the boys said 'We're coming'.

Peter replied 'Please stay here and I will phone you as soon as I have seen Mummy'.

He was out of the house and driving the car without realising it. The hospital was about fifteen minutes drive away. Trying to be calm, but driving faster than usual, he went straight to the casualty entrance.

He stated his name and the duty nurse showed him to a waiting room saying 'Dr

Wylies will come and speak to you shortly'.

A sense of foreboding came over Peter as the Doctor appeared. He said 'your wife is alive and her condition is stable but she is deeply unconscious.

We are carrying out tests and X-rays and until the results are known I cannot comment further'.

'May I see her?' asked Peter. The doctor took him to an observation room. Jane lay peacefully with no signs of injury, her soft skin a little pale but no more. Tubes and cables connected her to various graphs and dials.

The doctor said 'If you would like to sit with her please do so and if there is any change the monitoring equipment will automatically alert the nurse.

There is not much more I can do for now'.

Peter glanced at the green blips on the screen measuring vital functions. Jane was breathing steadily as if in a normal sleep.

After a few minutes sitting in the chair Peter remembered his sons would be waiting for his call. He walked along the corridor to a payphone and phoned the house.

The phone was answered instantly and he knew they would be sharing the phone.

Putting on a cheery voice he said 'It's OK boys, Mum has knocked herself out. Go on to bed, I'll stay here for a while. They will probably keep her in hospital to make sure she is OK. Goodnight'.

He did not allow time for their questions. Thomas the elder son looked at Josh and said 'Does he think we are that stupid? Still it is nearly midnight and we had better go to bed as he says'.

Peter returned to his chair at the bedside. He sat and gazed at his wife and tried to make her wake up by force of will.

At 3.30am the doctor returned. 'I suggest you go home to rest Mr Haynes and we will speak tomorrow. I hope to have some news about 10am'.

Peter drove back to the house. He checked the boys who were both sleeping soundly, made a pot of tea and sat in the kitchen until dawn.

CHAPTER 2

At 7.30 am he woke the boys and gave them breakfast. Father and children were quiet and trying unsuccessfully to make conversation. He took them to school and promised they could visit Mum that evening.

He returned to the hospital and waited for the doctor. Dr Wylies joined him and they went into the same little room. Jane looked exactly the same.

Dr Wylies looked serious as he spoke. 'Your wife has sustained brain damage and is in a coma. It is impossible to say when she will regain consciousness.'

Anticipating the next question he said 'When, and if, she regains consciousness we will not know the extent or the effect of her injuries'.

'What do you mean IF?' said Peter.

Dr Wylies replied 'I am sorry to be so blunt but modern practice dictates that we keep you fully informed. Something I do not always agree with. You look as though you have been up all night and I know it is a shock. Your wife is in expert care and I have been straight with you. She could just as easily make a full recovery'.

Peter, asking 'Should I sit and talk to her and play her music in an effort to reach her subconscious day after day?' Dr Wylies replied 'We have both heard of such stories but I think it's the visitor who gets comfort from this rather than the patient.'

'Think about it, we will accommodate you if you wish. I expect you will tire of the vigil after a few days, it is exhausting'.

'Thank you for your time, Doctor' said Peter. He sat by the bed calling on all his strength of character. His thoughts drifted back to his eighteenth birthday. He had sat awkwardly with his father and said 'Dad, I have made up my mind. I don't want to come in to the property development business. At least not yet. I want to see life a bit, maybe travel'. His father hid his feelings well. 'I understand, son'.

With typical determination Peter went down to the Army careers office the next day. The recruitment officer studied the 6' 3 rangy young man with shoulders like gallows and the jutting blue chin. He stood erect with a quiet but not shy demeanour.

'Do you have a regiment in mind that you would like to join?' 'No sir'. The officer said 'I am going to put you forward for the Coldstream Guards. You won't thank me for it at first but if you can stick it, it will set you up for life. You have entrance exams to take and fitness tests to do. What do you have to say?' Peter impassive, replied, 'Yes sir'.

After he had left, the recruitment officer talked to one of his colleagues. 'I had a potential Guards Officer in just now; it made my day. There's just something about him. I very nearly called him Sir'.

He did two years in the Coldstreams during which he had a spell in Northern Ireland and gave a good account of himself. Physically he filled out and the air of authority became more apparent as he was promoted.

At twenty-three years old he was called to Hereford for an interview. 'You know which regiment is based here, I take it?' The senior officer looked at him with eyes boring in to his soul. 'You have been selected to join the S.A.S. If you survive the training you will be a member of the best regiment in the world. The selection process is rigorous, the training unbelievable and the rewards are few. You won't be able to boast because you can't tell anybody anything. Very few men make the grade; if you don't, you will answer to me'.

During the training he was sent to the Brecon Beacons alone in the back of the truck. It was November. He weighed fifteen stones and he was given a rucksack that he heaved on to his back. The rucksack weighed eleven stones. The rain was steady and freezing cold. The mist was swirling and darkness falling. The truck stood there, engine running.

The Major said. 'You have your map and compass. I want you to meet this truck at the rendezvous on the map at 3 a.m.' The truck drove off in to the mist. Peter started trudging along the uneven ground. Rain running down his neck. The rucksack was cutting in to his shoulders.

He plodded on for as long as he could and then stopped to rest. Hungry and thirsty he opened the rucksack. It was full of bricks! He got up again and sucked some water off of the bushes. He called on his mental reserves and moved on. At ten minutes to three he spotted the truck and walked around to the back of it. A soldier sat there holding out a mug of tea. Peter unhitched the rucksack.

The soldier said 'Give me the map and compass, you won't need it any more'. Peter reached out for the mug. A voice in the darkness shouted. 'Off we go driver. Haines, be in Hereford Barracks ready for inspection at 8 a.m. If you are not there you have failed'. The truck disappeared in to the mist.

Peter got there and learned a lot about himself on the way. In particular, never give up. During his spell in the famous regiment, he saw all the action for which he was trained. He did things and saw things that a civilised human being should not be called upon to do. Afterwards, he joined the family firm but never lost the detached air about him that was as evident as the authority.

He settled into a routine of visits to the hospital, with the boys. Over the next few weeks, and although friends and relatives were keen at first, it was difficult to sit with a sleeping person for long.

Once or twice he looked at the life support machines and wondered guiltily, but concluded that where there is life there is hope. His hospital visits became fewer as he struggled to maintain life at home and work.

He began to wonder about the circumstances of the accident. Who was the other driver? Was he or she hurt?

One evening having returned from the hospital he was sitting alone in his study when the doorbell rang. Peter went to the door and opened it. A rather smart but casually dressed man in his early thirties said 'Hi, I'm Julian, can I have a word? It's about the car crash'. Peter took him to the study.

Julian was a charmer with good looks. He was probably athletic in his younger days although it appeared good living had taken its toll thought Peter wryly, as he spotted Julian was carrying a few extra pounds in weight.

Julian suddenly blurted out 'It was my driver who smashed into your wife's car and I have come to apologise and see if I can do anything'.

Peter asked 'Why doesn't your driver come himself?'

'He does as he's told' said Julian.

Curious, thought Peter. However he replied 'Tell me about the accident'.

Julian began 'We were coming down Winsley Hill a bit fast and my driver Barney drifted across the road on the left hander at the bottom of the hill and hit your wife's Mini on the offside. We were in a Range Rover that practically ran over the front of the Mini.'

Peter visualised the scene. 'Was Barney hurt?' he asked.

'Not a bit' said Julian. 'I was; bruised ribs, cuts on the legs, ruined my love life for a while! Anyway, I hear the wife is a bit incommunicado so now is your chance for a break. I have a villa and yacht in Spain and the address is in the envelope. Think about it but not for long, it will do you good'. Julian breezed out of the house.

CHAPTER 3

Peter sank weakly into his chair and looked at the envelope on the table. It was bulkier than at first appeared and although numbed by the brash intrusion of this 'man about town' he opened it.

Sure enough there was a postcard of Puerto Banus near Marbella showing a beautiful villa and an address written on the card. Also in the envelope was £5,000 in new £50 notes, still in the bank wrapper. A note unsigned said 'This will buy the ticket and a whole lot more when you arrive'.

Peter went to bed thinking - 'A stranger says abandon your hospital visits, take the money and have a holiday'. Two more different characters could not be conceived.

Peter, trained in his previous career to be very perceptive, turned over every word that Julian said and began to realise that something was wrong.

In the morning he dropped the boys at school and went straight to the Police Station.

He asked if PC Enfield was on duty. He was, and Peter re-introduced himself. 'Sorry sir' said PC Enfield 'I have attended a lot of accidents since that one'.

Peter said 'Do you mean to say that you were at the scene'. PC Enfield nodded. Peter continued 'Can you remember the Range Rover drifting over to the right into the path of my wife's Mini?'

'That's what the driver told you, is it?' asked PC Enfield and went on 'It's only fair to tell you that the driver has been charged with a drink driving offence and dangerous driving. His passenger, who appeared to be his employer, confirmed that the driver had drunk seven or eight whiskies'.

Peter said 'One last question - where are the cars?'

PC Enfield gave the address of the local recovery garage. Peter drove to the hospital but it was a duty call, nothing had changed. He went next to the garage recovery yard where crashed cars stood sadly side by side. His wife's little white Mini was there crushed up to the windscreen on the offside. He did not go close to it for fear of upsetting himself. He moved on to the Range Rover. At first glance the damage looked superficial, but closer inspection showed the front offside wheel pushed back into the footwell area jamming the clutch and brake pedals. There were spots of blood on the heel pad of the driver's carpet. The passenger side footwell was undamaged.

Peter had seen enough.

Driving back to the house he wondered how he could get to meet the driver called Barney. He did not want PC Enfield to know what he was thinking - yet.

That evening he had supper with the boys as usual and they spoke about their day. As usual he only half listened and wondered why he did not feel close to his family. This feeling of an outsider looking in occupied his thoughts more and more.

Darkness was falling and he suddenly made up his mind. 'Thomas, may I borrow your big torch please, I want to go out for a while'. Thomas knew better than to ask where he was going.

Peter returned to the crash recovery yard. All was in darkness. He studied the chain link fence and gates. Then he shook the gates making plenty of noise and immediately moved into the shadow. He stood motionless. No one came and no dogs barked. It was the only precaution he could think of taking. Reappearing, he climbed the gates and dropped into the yard.

He crept to the Range Rover and tried the passenger door. It was not locked. He climbed in and sat as if he was a passenger. Looking in the glove box he found what he was looking for. The garage service records for the vehicle.

Tucked in the booklet were some garage bills. He studied the bills and found more than he dared hope. 'RWR Mr Barnes 0626 864210'. 'Ring when ready' when the work is finished on the car. He pocketed the slip of paper.

Peter climbed out of the yard and drove thoughtfully back to the house. He sat in the study, poured himself a drink, and contemplated the next move. He dialled the number and said 'Is Mr Barnes there please?'

'Who wants him?' Came the guarded reply.

Peter thought quickly 'It is PC Evans of Wiltshire Police. PC Enfield asked me to call on you. He forgot to get you to sign part of your statement regarding the car crash.

Your case comes up shortly and we do not want an adjournment do we?'

'Yes we do' said Barney.

'Well' said Peter 'you don't want a senior policeman digging deeper into your affairs do you?

Barney said 'What's that supposed to mean?'

Peter, taking the initiative said 'Will you please give me directions to your house'.

He noted that Barney was not bright enough to realise he did not have the address.

Peter memorised the address and put the phone down.

It was 9pm. He called out to the boys and said 'I m going back out'. They knew he was up to something and they also knew he probably wouldn't tell them.

He followed the directions to a little village deeper into Wiltshire. Barney's home proved to be a small terraced house. Peter rang the bell and a heavily built man in an open neck shirt answered. Peter said 'I rang a short while ago'.

'Yeah' said Barney stepping out onto the pavement and glowering down at Peter.

This was a big and heavy man who looked tough in a bar room sort of way.

Peter played his ace card. 'You weren't driving the car that night'

'How did you find that out?' growled Barney.

'I wasn't certain until you just confirmed it' said Peter.

'You aren't a copper are you?'

'Can I come in for a drink?'

Barney did not answer but walked into the house. Without consulting Peter he took two cans of beer off the sideboard and threw one to Peter. He sat down and said 'I'm listening'.

Peter explained how he studied the accident as recounted by Julian and that he had examined the Range Rover. He concluded that the driver was injured by bruised ribs against the steering wheel and the cuts to his legs confirmed by the blood on the driver's side. He said that the front passenger was not injured. 'That was you Barney' said Peter.

'Now why did you swap places before the police arrived?

'What's it to you?' said Barney.

'It was my wife you drove into', said Peter, 'and she is now in a coma in hospital. I intend to get to the bottom of this Barney'.

'You can't prove any of it' said Barney. Peter responded 'Normally people want to avoid prosecution, not volunteer for it. You are a very loyal employee, it seems'.

'You won't go to jail for drink driving but you could for perverting the course of justice. Think about it Barney, you look like a man who likes his liberty'.

Barney did think for several minutes. 'What do you want me to do?'

Peter said 'Surprisingly little for the moment. What did Julian have on you to make you sit in his place?'

'Nothing' replied Barney, 'He said he would give me five grand'.

'You as well' said Peter. Barney looked puzzled. Peter continued. 'What is the job you have with Julian?

'Driver' replied Barney. 'And what good is a driver with no licence Barney?' It was evident that Barney hadn't thought of that.

Pressing home the advantage, Peter found that Barney was not too intelligent but had a loyalty to his boss. His role seemed to be that of a minder, come driver.

'Barny, what sort of business is Julian in?' asked Peter.

'I've been daft to talk to you' said Barney, 'Leave while you can still walk'. Peter left.

Driving home he reflected on events so far. It was evident that Julian could produce £5,000 to overcome any problem he encountered. Why did he need a heavyweight minder? This is Wiltshire, not Chicago. Still he had met local businessmen before, who felt it necessary to have muscle men alongside them, for no apparent reason.

CHAPTER 4

Over the next few days he settled back into the routine of visiting the hospital and looking after the boys. Although, with exams imminent, they were studying hard and were as preoccupied as him.

On his next visit to see Jane he asked to see Dr Wylies, who informed him there was no change. Peter remarked it was eight weeks since the accident. Dr Wylies reminded him it could be the same in eight months.

Peter asked if there was a point at which the doctors switched off the life support machine. 'No' came the very firm reply. He realised his question was premature to say the least. Humbled, Peter drove home. Gradually he formed his plan. He knew he could not concentrate on work until some questions were answered. Fortunately his building company was largely delegated and his foreman could be left to the day to day business. The occasional phone call would have to keep things ticking over at the office.

The next morning he took the boys to school as usual. He sat in the car until they went into class. Then he walked to the Headmasters Office and asked to see him. The Headmaster made sympathetic small talk. Peter interjected and asked if the boys could become boarders at short notice for a few weeks while Peter worked in Spain on a project.

The Headmaster was pleased to help but expressed concern over Mrs Haynes. Peter explained about Jane's coma and said he would be in constant touch. After all, Spain was only 2 or 3 hours away these days.

During the next few days he carried out the chores that involve shutting the house for a few weeks. He knew that Jane would have organised it in no time and was sure he would forget to cancel something.

He visited the travel agent and booked a flight to Malaga, one way. 'Aren't you coming back?' said the pretty young girl behind the counter.

Peter said he would, if only to see her again. She smiled. He asked if she could arrange car hire. 'Yes of course, any particular car you require?' 'Yes' he said ' a very particular car, right down to the colour'.

Undaunted, the girl said there were specialists in every field, and laughed. Within 3 days all was arranged. He explained to the boys that he had a chance to do some work abroad and have a break. He told them they were going to board at school. They jumped at the idea and he wondered what boarding was all about.

'Better not ask' he thought!

'Please visit the hospital boys; I know it's not easy but Mum may know you are there even if she cannot respond. Keep in touch with your grandparents; they will carry on visiting Mum.

In an emergency the Headmaster knows how to contact me but I will obviously keep in touch'.

He called at the hospital and kissed his wife telling her he would soon be back. Not even a flicker of an eyelash did he get in return.

CHAPTER 5

He left a note, on the hall table, of the address he had been given in Spain and drove on to Lulsgate airport near Bristol. He parked his car and unloaded his luggage.

On checking in, the security guard took special interest in his rucksack and decided he was a serious camper. He had told his sons he would camp to keep the cost down and they had enjoyed advising him on what to take. For once he showed tact and let them make their suggestions. Although with his survival training there was not much for him to learn.

Two and a half hours later he walked out of Malaga airport into the scorching heat of the afternoon sun. He looked at the details on his car hire charge form. It was a smaller office than the ones of the usual car hire companies. Formalities were exchanged and his licence studied. In poor English the car hire representative asked him to take good care of his brand new addition to the fleet. A box of provisions was handed to him as arranged.

Outside the office stood over a ton of Nissan Patrol 4 wheel drive, resplendent in the colour of desert sand. Extra tanks were strapped to the front bumper, a front winch and shovels on the bonnet. The Desert Dueler tyres still showed their manufacturing marks.

The vehicle looked too good to use. Peter ignored the feeling that he was just going back to his army days in the Jeep. You never know what you might need, he said silently to himself.

He climbed into the unfamiliar left hand drive seat and started the big diesel. He moved out into the traffic and followed the coast road towards Marbella. He had studied a map before leaving home and knew that Pureto Banus was the other side of Marbella.

When the sign said 'Marbella 2 Kilometres', he pulled off left on the underpass and headed inland. Within minutes he was out of the built up area and climbing into the hills. He drove on for a half an hour and stopped the Nissan on a bend with a spectacular view down the hills to the sea.

Stepping out, he realised the luxury of air conditioning. It was still very hot although the sun was low in the sky. He restarted and looked for a suitable track off the road.

He turned off and began a steep winding climb up the track for about 15 minutes. At a clearing he drove off the track and set up camp. He knew that putting up the tent and generally making himself comfortable would take a while, as he had not camped for a long time. He erected the two man tent and laid out his sleeping bag inside.

Ignoring the small gas stove he made a small fire and cooked a simple meal of eggs and beans, and made a cup of coffee, using the water from one of the jerry cans on the front bumper of the Nissan.

Feeling rather smug about his aptitude for camping, he planned his movements for the next day. Dusk was falling and he decided to have a very early night and lay in the tent and thought about the events that brought him this far.

At dawn he skipped breakfast, made coffee and struck camp, his restlessness getting the better of him. He paused to wonder if his wife's condition had changed.

How were the boys? Did he really miss the family? Why was it more important to unravel the mystery surrounding Julian? Part of his thinking was to spend time in isolation, miles from anywhere, to untangle his thoughts.

With this in mind he started the Nissan and looked up the track. In the distance he saw the beginning of the Sierra Morena Mountains. As good a way as any, he thought. He started the climb and the deep ruts in the track made the underside of the Nissan brush the centre of the track. He drove carefully and slowly as the climb steepened.

Late morning he stopped where the track cut through a bank, to have a drink and let the Nissan cool down.

Once again he marvelled at the air conditioning, for outside it was searingly hot with not so much as a whiff of a breeze. The only sound was the constant chirping of the cicadas. He sat in the shade of the Nissan and decided he would make a more permanent camp at the next level clearing.

CHAPTER 6

Suddenly he heard a low groan, an animal perhaps, a wild boar grunt. He listened intently; could it be human? All his senses were tuned in. The short hairs on his neck prickled. His muscles tensed as he moved his weight onto his toes, his fingers rigid to deal the chopping blow he had not used in years. His training took over and anyone at home who thought they knew him would not have recognised him now. He was never proud of his past in the Army and did not speak of it.

On impulse he started walking up the track, around the bend, listening all the time.

There he saw it. An old Fordson Major tractor completely upside down. Red, and red with rust, it stood on its steering wheel and huge rear wheels.

Pinned beneath the steering wheel was the source of the groan. A man spread-eagled on the ground, the steering wheel hub centred in his chest, one leg showing blood through old torn trousers.

Peter dived down and slithered towards the face. The sweat and stubble mingled with dirt. The lips were cracked and dry and blood trickling from the corner of the mouth.

Peter whispered 'Are you all right?' The big Spaniard rolled his eyes and moved his head slightly from side to side. Then in a loud clear voice that made Peter jump, 'Of course I am not all right, there is a great weight upon my chest, stupid English'.

Peter looked closer; the weather beaten swarthy skin, the peasant farmer clothes. Surely a local farmer, but speaking English? 'What is your name?' asked Peter.

'I am pinned here beneath my tractor and you say, what eeze your name? It is Manuel, OK?'

'What else,' thought Peter? He said 'I have a big Nissan with a winch down the track, stay there while I get it'.

'I cannot go anywhere' sighed Manuel.

He ran back down the track to the Nissan. Seeing the steep bank alongside, he backed down the track to where the bank was shallow. Selecting four wheel drive and low ratio gears he turned to the bank. The vehicle began the climb. Peter estimated he was at 45 degrees, he could only see the clear blue sky. Onwards and upwards he went, feeling as though the Nissan would fall over backwards at any moment.

Suddenly he was falling forward. In a split second he realised he had not checked to see what was at the top of the bank. A precipice? A long roll in the vehicle to the bottom of a ravine? No! He bounced down onto level ground, rock strewn scrubland, but level ground.

He gathered his wits and began to weave slowly between the boulders to stop above the tractor and Manuel. He turned at right angles to the track and jumped out of the Nissan and released the winch cable. Pulling the cable behind him he scrambled down the bank. Looping the cable around the front axle of the tractor he ran to the winch control and took up the slack cable.

Back to Manuel, he went down on hands and knees and said 'I will winch the tractor up a little and the back wheels of the tractor will act as a pivot. Lie still and

I will ease you out from under the tractor'.

He went up the bank and operated the winch. The front bumper of the Nissan dipped slightly as the cable took the strain. As planned the front of the tractor lifted clear of Manuel. Peter knew he must be injured internally by the blood from his mouth. As he started back down the bank he stared in astonishment. Manuel practically jumped to his feet and stretched to his full height. Peter shouted 'Your chest - your ribs! You are bleeding internally'. Manuel said 'I do not think so, my lips are cracked and dry and that is where the blood is from. My chest is bruised but it's nothing, not all the weight was upon me'.

'And your leg?' said Peter. 'Just scratches from the scrub bushes' said Manuel.

'How long were you there?' Peter asked. 'Long enough to be thirsty' replied Manuel.

'Sorry' said Peter and went back to the Nissan for his water bottle. He approached Manuel to hand him the bottle. It was the first time he had stood at the same level as Manuel. This Spaniard must be over 6'6" with a great barrel of a chest. His hand took the bottle and dwarfed it, almost hiding it. Peter judged him to be about 35 years old, very heavy, but it was not fat. A very rough looking individual, yet impeccable English even if heavily accented.

Peter said 'I do not understand. You are a hill farmer, yet you speak English so well'.

Manuel replied 'I went to University in Madrid. I was enjoying the study of English and travelled to your country as well. Later my father died and left me the farm. I thought I would try the farming life and I enjoy it. Meanwhile I practice the English as much as possible by visiting the bars and restaurants along the coast as my hobby'.

All of this was spoken in halting style with pauses while he searched for the correct words. Peter should have anticipated the question 'What are you doing on this track? It leads only to my farm' said Manuel.

Peter said 'I like to take my holidays alone in quiet places'. Manuel looked puzzled but said nothing.

He did however look lovingly at his tractor and remarked 'My tractor must return the right way up or my wife will be angry'.

Peter soon winched it right over on to its wheels. The fuel and oil had drained out and long since soaked into the ground. Manuel said 'If you will tow me to the farm I will in turn provide refreshment'.

CHAPTER 7

Peter manoeuvred the Nissan further up the track and reversed back. He found the unused hemp towrope in the Nissan and connected up to the tractor.

Manuel hoisted his considerable bulk up on to the tractor and smiled as if in heaven.

They set off slowly in formation and bumped along the track for nearly an hour.

The farm was like so many in Spanish Sierras. Small, poor, held together with love and hard work but little else. Chickens, a goat and a donkey all scratched around in the yard as Peter towed in the tractor.

A short stocky woman looked out over the stable type door from the kitchen. Manuel called out 'My tractor, she broke down and my new friend Peter helped me'. Then there followed a boisterous exchange in Spanish.

Peter concluded that the English report was for his benefit. It became apparent that Manuel's wife did not speak English. This Spanish farmer could teach some of Peter's friends a few things about good manners to strangers.

Manuel led Peter into the kitchen. It was cool and dark and a step backwards in time.

Various vegetables were hanging from the ceiling. Red and green peppers, onions and strange articles that may be edible to the Spanish, thought Peter.

The two men sat at a scrubbed pine table. Manuel's wife was introduced as Maria.

She proceeded to lay the table, an earthenware pitcher full of red wine; heavy home cooked bread, large onions, cheese and olives. Two thick misshapen glass tumblers appeared and Manuel poured. Maria brought a jug of water.

Peter was interested in wine and wondered if he was about to make a discovery. He did! Instead of a rustic throat burner the wine was smooth and fruity. Manuel showed Peter how to enjoy the wine then take a sip of water.

He then picked up an onion and started munching it like an apple. They laughed as Peter followed suit with eyes watering. He went quiet as he realised he had not laughed in months. Guilt came over him as he thought of the situation at home. A large hand settled on his arm and Manuel said. 'I am your friend; you are no longer alone. Let's eat'. They talked and ate and drank.

Much later Manuel led Peter to an upstairs room and Peter collapsed on to the bed fully clothed, exhausted and a little drunk. His last thoughts were, Jane, the boys and then Julian. Thoughts became dreams and mystery swirled in his mind.

When he woke it was already hot and he walked delicately downstairs. Maria gave him a gravelly cup of strong black coffee. He walked outside and Manuel was replenishing the tractor with oil and fuel.

Coming straight to the point, Manuel said 'I expect you will want to carry on your holiday straight away. However you know where I am and you know I am a good man in a crisis if you get into one'. Peter studied the bulging muscles and jutting chin and smiled to himself.

He said his good byes and drove off in a now dusty Nissan. Back down the track and on to the winding mountain road. In the distance the sea shimmered and he stopped again high above Puerto Banus.

Unsure of his next plan he resumed the drive into the busy five-way junction just outside the harbour. He drove slowly into the harbour area where some of the world's most expensive yachts are moored. Famous people and people who want to be famous, make for this area like others head for Mecca.

Peter drove slowly into a parking space among Porsches and Ferraris. He locked the car and walked past the waterside restaurants until he found a table close to the promenading people. The table was impeccably laid and a smart waiter looked at him with disdain.

Peter glanced at himself. He had slept in his clothes. His once light blue shirt was stained with sweat and dust from yesterday's rescue of Manuel. He had not showered. A mess of a man in a very smart restaurant in one of the world's most fashionable resorts. He tried to explain to the waiter that things are not always what they seem.

The waiter was not convinced; could he show he was able to pay?

Peter gave him some Euro notes and said he would like to have a shower and change of clothes, which were in the Nissan visible from where he sat. 'Is this possible?'

'In Puerto Banus if you can pay, everything is possible' said the waiter. Peter repeated the bribe. He fetched his change of clothes and followed the waiter to the rooms behind the restaurant. He shaved, showered, changed, and returned to his table. He noticed ruefully that the waiter talked in different languages to other customers. Is it only the English who speak one language? He thought.

Peter asked that if the table was not required, could he sit there and observe the local scene. 'No problem' said the waiter. 'Shall I bring you a drink?

'A beer please'.

'By the way, do you happen to know Julian Wilding?' said Peter. 'Yes' said the waiter 'That's his yacht' pointing to a beautiful craft. 'Do you know him?' 'Not yet' replied Peter.

Discreetly the waiter withdrew. In the private quarters he dialled a number and said 'Someone is enquiring about Mr Wilding. He is sat at one of the front tables in an orange shirt'.

Peter ate a leisurely meal and watched the passers by. He did not notice a tourist taking photos like so many others. The 'tourist' returned to the yacht and reported to Mr Wilding. The Polaroid picture, already developed, showed Peter at the table.

Julian pondered for a moment, then, yes he recognised the face. The husband from the car crash caper back in Wiltshire.

CHAPTER 8

He had expected to see Peter turn up.
Five thousand in your hand and a promise of a good time in Spain? No trouble
from the wife? Chance of a lifetime! Yet
something is wrong. Why did Peter sit and
watch the scene? Why not ask around and
head straight for him? Still maybe he's
overawed and adjusting his mind from
his mundane life. He'll turn up when he's
ready.

Peter did not turn up that day. As the
sun went down he paid his restaurant bill
and thanked the waiter for the use of the
shower.

He walked over to the Nissan and noticed a dent in the front wing. 'A pity on
any new vehicle, whether its mine or not'
thought Peter. However there was a note
under the windscreen wiper.

'I suppose no one could just drive off
without admitting to it' he thought. He
opened the folded note that said 'The
people watching me write this note think

I am leaving my name and address, you and I know different!'

'Comedian' said Peter out loud. He climbed in and drove out of Puerto Banus as the evening revellers were coming in. Somehow he was pleased to move away from the ritzy scene. On his way from the harbour he saw the night lights on Julian's yacht.

Coloured bulbs from stem to stern and on the stern deck a gathering of well-dressed men and young girls were enjoying cocktails.

'I suppose it depends what you want out of life' thought Peter. He began to wonder about the lifestyle and how Julian made his money. One thing's for certain, he certainly lives well!

He stopped outside the telephone booths where the staff still help you make your call.

The miracle of satellite telecommunications meant he was soon talking to the hospital.

The nurse said there was no change but that is not necessarily bad news.

He called the school next. The housemaster said the boys had settled in well and were working for exams. He would tell them Father had phoned.

He drove out of town, heading for the hills. 'Why does life seem unreal? My family are thousands of miles away and I should be there supporting them. Have I run away?

I think not. Someone should find out about this man, Julian Wilding. Do I want justice or vengeance?'

He made up his mind to just get to know Julian a bit and let things develop. On and on he drove, quietly and thoughtful. Darkness had fallen. In the dark he missed the turning for Manuel's track to the farm and had not consciously been heading back.

'I am not capable of erecting the tent in the dark' he said aloud. He pulled off the road on to rough ground and away from the glare of occasional headlights. Climbing into the rear of the Nissan he folded the rear seats down and moved his luggage to one side. He locked the doors and slid into the sleeping bag. 'Some camper I am' he smiled.

He spent a fitful and uncomfortable night but again planned the day ahead.

CHAPTER 9

At first light he climbed out and stretched his stiff limbs. He drew some water from the container on the front of the Nissan and washed and shaved. Cold water shaving is not to be recommended he thought as the razor scraped reluctantly over his chin.

He unpacked a short-sleeved white shirt and dark blue slacks and moccasins. Feeling clean and tidy he drove back to Puerto Banus. This time he parked in the big public car park and walked to the harbour. The morning was clean and fresh and he felt hungry.

A constitutional walk around the harbour was called for, passing the fabulous yachts.

Yachts from Jersey, Panama, Cayman Isles and any other tax haven, Peter observed wryly. All were silent and deserted at this time of day. He walked to the other end of the almost enclosed harbour, past his restaurant of the previous evening.

There were several fast looking boats on dry land. They did not look old but were damaged or burnt or both. He left the harbour wall and jumped down onto the sandy beach. The beach hut staff were just coming to life, although compared to the beach huts at Weymouth this was a four star beach hut he observed.

A suntanned young chap said 'You up early or just going home?' 'Up early' said Peter. 'Well then join me for a coffee'. They shook hands and introduced themselves.

The youngster said he was Jim and from Gloucester. Peter asked how he knew he was English. 'You look it' said Jim. They exchanged small talk for a while.

Peter said 'What happened to those boats at this end of the harbour?' Jim replied 'They are drug-running boats doing the fast trip from here to Gibraltar and back. There is a well-organised night run but if they are caught the boats are confiscated with the drugs haul. As you can see they do not always come quietly. Still it pays well - look at those big yachts'. Peter thanked Jim for the coffee. 'Any time' smiled Jim.

Peter walked back to the harbour wall and walked along in front of the shops past 'his' restaurant and around to the deep water where the fabulous yachts were. There were six in all and Julian's was flanked by two even bigger ones. However, all things are relative, and Julian's must be one hundred and fifty feet long.

Peter selected a wooden seat and sat and watched the activity on the other yachts.

The bigger ones had permanent staff on the stern, one on duty on the gangplank, one stood under the shade of the upper deck.

On the stern deck of one yacht two girls in waitress uniform were laying a table for twelve. Napkins matched the sunshade awnings. A huge display of yellow roses matched the napkins. Orange juice and champagne stood in ice buckets.

As he watched, a white Rolls Royce pulled up. Nothing could be seen through the very dark windows, and nothing happened for a few minutes. Then at a precise moment the gangplank officer stepped forward and opened the door of the Rolls. A man of Arabic appearance stepped out in flowing white robes. A lady complete with veil followed him. Not a word was spoken and they glided below decks.

Peter was almost relieved to see that it was just oil money that funded this lifestyle. He knew it was unlikely that they would associate with the Europeans alongside. The Arab culture was not new to him and his thoughts went back to desert skirmishes.

He was almost unaware that a man had joined him on the seat. He said 'Its time you told me you've arrived'.

Peter's jaw dropped as he recognised Julian. 'Sorry, I was a bit taken aback by all this' he lied. Julian laughed. 'Well come aboard 'Paradise', we are about to have breakfast'.

The breakfast was a similar layout to that on the bigger yacht. One girl was laying the table, but dressed in jeans and a T-shirt. The floral display was limited to vases of flowers.

Julian introduced Peter to two men, Danny and Tony. Both men were in their early thirties and looked fit and tanned. Julian said, 'Technically they are employees but I tell them most people would pay me to help on this boat'. They both laughed dutifully.

Julian asked where Peter was staying. 'At a farm in the hills above here'. Peter thought he would be teased if he admitted he was camping.

They sat down to breakfast and Peter was delighted to be served an English breakfast.

They all relaxed and got acquainted. Peter remembered that this was the man who caused the car accident, and here he was making friends.

A frown spread over his face. Danny said 'Are you OK? You look a little serious for a man on holiday'.

Peter apologised and said his wife was in hospital and he felt guilty being away.

Julian exclaimed 'Peter I am so sorry, I haven't even asked how she is'. No thought Peter and I know insincerity when I hear it. Concern was quickly shown and another subject found.

Julian said 'Would you like to look around the boat?' On finishing breakfast they went 'forward'. The stateroom was at sea level. There were huge sofas around a full size Chinese rug. A large butlers' table at knee height was in the centre of the rug with two soft buckskin armchairs facing it. In one corner was a 'baby grand electric piano'. The effect was a cool and expensive room of taste.

There were guest cabins, each with a colour theme, so that they could be referred to by colour. Each had an en suite shower. The cabins were arranged three on each side of the gangway.

Julian said 'My cabin is further forward' but that was all. He went nimbly up a stepladder to the bridge. Peter followed and was confronted with all the electronic gadgetry that adorns modern yachts. They each sat in the 'deck chairs' as Julian laughingly called them. Actually they were leather, fully adjustable seats that one sees in executive saloon cars.

Through the long sloping windscreen he looked across the harbour and imagined the spray flying from the bows as they put to sea. Julian said 'Do I detect a longing to put to sea?' 'Yes in a word' Peter replied. 'And so we shall' said Julian.

They left the bridge and went below decks to the engine room. Peter always interested in engines, was impressed by the immense twin turbo charged diesels in gleaming white. Julian explained that they were American Caterpillar engines tuned to provide a top speed in excess of 30 knots.

'There are of course crew quarters, galley and less interesting parts of the boat, but that's a quick tour for now' said Julian.

They returned to the stern deck where Danny and Tony were putting the finishing touches to the breakfast table floral display that seemed to be obligatory on these yachts.

Julian said 'If you will forgive me I am expecting some business associates shortly and am going to my cabin to prepare the agenda'. Peter took the hint and said he should go. Julian said 'Go where? I invited you down here and expect you to stay on board or with me at the villa. Did you not realise?'

Peter said 'In that case I will need to go up to the farm for my luggage. It won't take long'. Julian said 'Be back in time for lunch aboard at 2 o'clock when I will be free, and maybe the other business pals can join us.

'Danny will ride with you for company'. This last part was a statement, not an offer.

CHAPTER 10

Danny and Peter walked around to the Nissan and drove up the now familiar road and took the track to the farm. On the way they exchanged small talk but that was all.

Manuel was tending his tractor that seemed to need constant attention. He was delighted to see Peter and shook hands reservedly with Danny. Peter said 'I have come for my luggage as I have been invited to stay on Mr Wilding's yacht'.

'Of course' said Manuel 'Come in'. As soon as they were inside Manuel said

'What luggage?' 'I know I did not leave any; can you put some clothes in a bag for me to carry out to the car'. Manuel delegated this to his wife.

Peter said 'Do you know Danny?' 'Only that the local Police think he may be involved in the fast boats trafficking drugs into Puerto Banus' said Manuel.

'That is why I asked' said Peter. Manuel explained that the local Police were his friends and that Puerto Banus was really only a village where everyone knew what went on. Peter said 'So, now you know where I am staying'. 'Yes' said Manuel 'and I do not like the company you keep. Maybe I misjudged you'.

Peter said 'You did not; I am here to study Julian Wilding and his yacht. Now let's go out. Act normally and put the bags in the car'.

Maria had given Danny a can of Coke and they were talking in slow Spanish. 'You travel light' observed Danny. They don't miss a trick thought Peter.

Suddenly Manuel said 'I must come to town in the morning, maybe we could meet for a coffee Peter'.

Arrangements were made and Peter murmured under his breath 'I owe you an explanation Manuel'.

Peter and Danny made the return journey. Without being too obvious Peter asked questions about Julian. Danny said he did not get involved in Julian's business but he dealt a lot in investments and 'had his fingers in a lot of pies'. Somewhere he has acquired a lot of hard cash, thought Peter.

Peter padded out the conversation with small talk but realised Danny was too quick thinking to give anything away.

It was 1pm when they arrived at the harbour. Danny said 'We can freshen up before lunch on the Paradise'. Peter took a clean shirt and toilet bag to a guest cabin marked 'Blue'. Danny said 'Give me the shirt and I will have it ironed while you shower'.

As Peter was dressing a knock at the cabin door proved to be the return of his shirt by a delightful young Spanish girl. Shy and embarrassed, she handed the immaculate shirt to him. 'Appearance is everything' said Danny from the gangway.

They returned to the aft deck where again the table was laid. Tony handed them iced fruit cocktail drinks. Both he and Danny had changed clothes and looked cool in the midday sun. Julian emerged from below decks with two Spanish gentlemen, one of whom carried a brief case. Introductions all round and more drinks. Danny and Tony chose more soft drinks. As Peter selected a gin and tonic he said 'You make me feel like an alcoholic'. Tony said 'The real professionals don't drink'. What 'professionals' was not clear although both he and Danny looked very fit he noticed once more.

The two Spaniards spoke good English and the conversation was about villas and golf courses. It was soon clear that Julian had bought a villa that morning. He said he might ask them to sell his existing villa in due course. After lunch the Spaniards rose, thanked Julian, rather indiscreetly, for payment and one of them produced a pair of handcuffs and snapped one around the handle of the briefcase and the other half around his wrist.

'You must be careful with all these tourists about' one said.

'Is there much crime in this area?' asked Peter nonchalantly.

'If there is, it goes largely undetected because so many of the Police are open to bribes' said Julian.

'What is the world coming to' laughed Danny. Peter studied each face as he dropped his bombshell of a question but no one had moved a muscle.

Julian said 'We are having a small party this evening and you would be our guest of honour if you are willing'.

Peter 'Yes please' and could he go into town and to the beach during the afternoon like a real holidaymaker.

Julian said 'You are here to relax and enjoy yourself. Come and go as you please.

Danny, you may join him, get your shorts and suntan oil'.

CHAPTER 11

They wandered around and studied the girls on the beach. Later in the afternoon they swam in the sea. It was evident that Danny enjoyed his company and was quite open in conversation except where Julian was concerned. He was the navigation officer he said, although as most sailings were at night he used radar more than the charts. He also said that Tony was the engineer but the yacht was so new, maintenance was minimal.

Peter mentioned how fit they both were and Danny said Julian required that they keep in shape and have a certain knowledge of unarmed combat.

'It suits his image and he feels safer. If Julian takes to you, as he has us, he will probably offer you some kind of job. He always surrounds himself with his friends who are very loyal'.

All these snippets of information Peter stored away whilst he built a picture.

Danny said 'When we return to the yacht I recommend you have a lie down as the party will go on all night. Do you have any evening clothes?' 'No' said Peter.

'Leave it to me' said Danny, 'We are about the same size. I guess cash is a bit tight back home?'

'Yes, what with a mortgage and school fees'.

While Peter was resting, Danny repeated the conversation to Julian in his stateroom.

'Right' said Julian 'If he is short of money we will soon corrupt his holier than thou attitude. Ensure he looks the part and make sure one of the girls singles him out for special attention tonight'.

Early in the evening Danny tapped the Blue Cabin door, entered, and laid clothes on the bed.

'I can't fault the service' said Peter. He shaved and showered; everything was provided, including aftershave.

He eagerly put on the clothes provided, feeling a little self conscious in the black bow tie. Two nights ago he had slept in his clothes. He liked the white evening jacket and noted the polished shoes.

Walking to the aft deck he noticed that the party lights were on and the moon was shining. Lights on the other boats shone on the faces of the envious holidaymakers strolling around the harbour.

He walked to the table and collected a cocktail. A Spanish girl came over to him and placed a pink carnation in his buttonhole. As she reached up to him, her perfume wafted by. Her olive skin positively glowed in the lights. Her dark hair lay heavily to her shoulders and a yellow carnation adorned it.

'There now, we both have a flower'. She whispered in his ear. Her green silk dress made a swishing noise as she moved and her figure was obvious beneath it. She smiled and said 'See you later'.

A voice from behind said 'I see you have made an impression already'. Julian continued, 'Just mingle and enjoy yourself, there are local dignitaries and business acquaintances here. We bring in girls from an agency just to oil the wheels of commerce. More business is done on these yachts than in the whole town'.

Peter did not learn much from the light hearted conversations and wished for the

company of Manuel who was more intelligent than some of the local 'dignitaries!'

However, he made the evening pass
pleasantly beneath the stars and was careful not to drink too much so that he could
stay on full alert. Around 11.30pm little
'Miss Green Dress' reappeared at his
arm.

She said 'Please show me around this
beautiful yacht'. Peter thought cynically, I
bet she could show me.

They passed through the stateroom.
There were people there but they were
restrained and behaving themselves, although he noted that whilst the men
were of various ages all the women were
young.

As they walked towards the Blue room,
Peter made up his mind. He climbed the
steps to the bridge and sat in the Captains
Chair. The girl sat puzzled in the other
chair, her gorgeous legs crossed and shoes
kicked off.

He said 'You are very desirable but I
want to remain loyal to my wife and children. I hope you will understand'.

She said 'I am very pleased there are
men like you'. Peter said 'Tell me about
yourself'. They talked for ages about her

family, her ambitions, and the necessity, as she saw it, to be an Escort girl. They looked at the stars and the glowing lights on the instrument panel of the yacht. Childlike she said 'We have our own stars on board ship'. She leaned towards him and his moral intentions began to weaken. Her full red lips brushed his cheek and she took his hand and led him away.

Meanwhile, back in the stateroom, Julian asked after Peter.

Tony said he was last seen going to the guest cabins with one of the girls. Julian thought 'Now he is one of the gang. He likes the high life and will carry out the occasional job'.

As dawn began to lighten the sky, Peter escorted his girl back to the harbour wall and said his goodbyes just like several others.

He didn't ask her name but would always remember the time they had shared. Julian looked satisfied at the fond farewells. Some of the other guests would need reminding of favours given tonight when they were reluctant to help deals along. With Peter, he hoped that the taste of tonight would be enough.

Peter returned to his cabin and was soon in bed. His frustrations and worries seemed to have stepped ashore with the girl. Would guilt pursue him he wondered as sleep took over.

CHAPTER 12

It was gone 10am when he woke and he had promised to meet Manuel at 11am. He dressed quickly and went aft. Tony was the only one on deck until Peter joined him for coffee. He said he was going to meet his farm friend and Tony just nodded.

He went to Jimmy's beach hut as arranged and Manuel was already there. 'Talk about a miracle' exclaimed Peter. Manuel had shaved and put on a bright red shirt and clean jeans and suede desert boots.

His thick black hair was shiny and pushed back over his ears. He looked like a well-scrubbed choirboy who had kept on growing.

For privacy they strolled along the seashore and Peter told Manuel of the events that brought him to Puerto Banus. 'What will you do next?' asked Manuel. Peter said that if there was anything illegal going on he would like to be instrumental in bringing Julian to justice. This was the best way of teaching him a lesson.

Manuel said 'I have not been idle since I saw you and I must warn you that Julian Wilding is not as harmless as you might think. It is believed he is a drug runner. His boat has been stopped three times at night and searched, each time nothing was found and he says that he likes to cruise the bay while entertaining. The last time he was stopped he complained to the authorities and they have promised him no further inconvenience.

One evening recently a local man picked a fight with your Mr Wilding but he would not get out of his chair at the Waterfront restaurant. Apparently he just smiled, and as the local went to dive on him, Julian's two men lifted him up in the air and threw him in the harbour. Unfortunately his head hit a small wooden dinghy and he died. No one wanted to be a witness and the Police were not interested. Julian did not leave his seat and finished his meal'.

All this was conveyed in Manuel's careful slow English, which helped Peter to picture the scene.

Peter said he would like to keep in touch and any more information would be welcome. They parted company and Peter walked back along the harbour to the telephone booths. He dialled the hospital and spoke to the nurse. 'No there was no change but wait, I have a surprise for you'. Thomas, his elder son, came on the line 'How are you Dad?' then let all his news out in a rush. Then Josh came on and did the same.

Peter asked why they were at the hospital. 'It's Sunday, Dad' said Josh. He listened to their voices rather than what they were saying and when they said goodbye he felt the tears welling up. He swallowed hard and walked back to the beach. He sat for a while just watching the sea. Later, he walked back towards the yacht. Still thinking about his sons. 'They seem happy enough and Jane is no worse'.

Julian was sat on deck with Danny and Tony and he joined them. They asked if he enjoyed the party and grinned.

Danny said 'How is Manuel? I was impressed by his English and would have thought he would want more from life than a small farm'. Peter detected they were expecting a righteous reply but he saw the trap. 'He seems happy enough' Peter said non-commitally.

Julian said 'Come on you two' looking in Danny and Tony's direction 'Lets get this old tub shipshape. I think an evening cruise is called for.' 'Would you like that?' he said to Peter. Peter replied 'Ooh yes please' like a child on a trip round the bay.

Then Julian said 'Let's talk awhile. You seem to have taken to this life style and I wonder if I could use you in my business. What is your speciality?' Peter replied 'I am a builder, I just work from home'. He saw no reason to mention his modest property portfolio.

'Right' said Julian 'That's easy I want to expand my construction business in Marbella and you could run that for me'.

'I don't speak the language' said Peter 'Besides I have a wife and family'.

Julian said 'Look I am not Father Christmas and many men would jump at the chance.

You will soon learn the language, and anyway, English is widely spoken. Your job would be to co-ordinate things and answer to me. If the idea appeals we will talk terms'.

'I will see to it that you fly home frequently and the pay will be substantial'.

'Meanwhile lets prepare for sea'.

They both returned to the bridge and Julian started the big diesels. After various checks and revs, the throbbing note of power on a short leash, reduced to a murmur.

Julian explained the dials and switches as he went through his routine. On the fore deck, crew, Peter had not seen before, were bringing in fenders and coiling ropes.

The electrically operated gangplank was retracted and Julian spoke into the ship to shore radio.

'Whisky 2 calling Puerto Banus. We are preparing to leave harbour for a pleasure cruise. We expect to return at 5am tomorrow'.

The harbourmaster acknowledged and wished them 'Good sailing'.

Julian said 'That is just a courtesy so that a patrolling gunboat does not blow us out of the water'. 'Why would that happen?' asked Peter.

Julian said 'Come off it Peter, you have asked enough questions around here to know that drug trafficking is rife'. Peter said 'Are you involved?

Julian replied ' If I was I would not tell you, but let's say anyone in business here is influenced by the trade and the money it brings. Let me ask you, if I was, how would you feel?'

'Having seen what money can buy here I could be swayed'. Peter lied.

Julian spoke into the deck hailer 'Let go forward', and a crewman slipped the bow mooring rope. 'Let go aft'. The winches began to wind in the ropes. Julian eased the twin throttles forward and they began to glide forward. When they were clear of the yachts flanking them he showed Peter how it was possible to turn the yacht on its own axis by putting one engine astern. The yacht turned sharply to pass the pontoon protecting the harbour. The pontoon was packed with holidaymakers with their cameras and kids.

'Watch this' said Julian. He flicked on the party lights and gave a cheeky blast on the horn. The bystanders waved and cheered. 'One of these days we will give some of them a ride'.

They slid out of the harbour in incredible quiet and into the night. Gradually the yacht picked up speed and the bows lifted. There was a bit of a swell but the yacht cut through the waves without rolling. In the cockpit area, which Julian always called the bridge; the green lights of the instrument panels were glowing. The radar was making its monotonous sweep and the depth gauge showed the fathoms beneath the keel.

Julian said 'If there is any malfunction we get a warning buzzer and we have automatic pilot as well. I don't use the autopilot much, as I like to feel in charge'.

While Peter wondered at the technology, the Spanish girl, he last saw laying the breakfast table, brought drinks to the bridge.

'Pinkers' said Julian 'I like the right drink for the right occasion'.

The girl placed their pink gin in the gimball holders made for the purpose.

On into the night they sailed and chatted about the sea and the stars. Julian said 'If I am entertaining, Danny will take the helm. He is a qualified navigator, which is comforting. Incidentally, Tony is an accomplished cook and I thought when you are ready we would eat in the stateroom, buffet style. I always leave it to Tony to surprise us'.

Peter asked 'How fast are we going?' 'About 12 knots' said Julian. Then he spoke into the intercom saying 'I am going to increase speed'. He pushed the 2 chrome throttle levers forward and Peter felt the push in his back, just like a sports car accelerating. The bows lifted and spray flew past the cockpit windows. Further forward the levers went and the yacht gradually levelled out to horizontal. The mighty roar of the diesels was evident but still there was no need to shout.

Peter asked 'Why the change from the bows up position'. Julian explained 'We are on the plane. That is to say the hull is now out of the water and we are just skimming the waves'. The speed indicators showed 25 knots and the rev counters near 4,000 revs. Julian eased the speed down to 12 knots and Tony in the galley said 'I am glad that little demonstration is over'.

Julian said 'We use about 20 gallons of diesel an hour normal running but fast cruising can double that. Look beyond the port bow and you can see the lights of Malaga'. The lights were twinkling like stars and a jet was making a beeline for the airport where Peter had landed only a few days ago.

Julian called to Danny to take the helm and Danny dutifully appeared. 'Down to the stateroom for a snack' said Julian.

CHAPTER 13

A small banquet was laid on the butler's table. Julian walked to the bar in the corner of the stateroom where Tony was sipping from a wine glass. There was a quick discussion and Julian approved the Sancerre wine chilled ready for inspection. 'This will complement the lobster nicely'. He moved over to the electronic piano and an invisible pianist started playing the muted tones of Chopin's Nocturne Number Two.

Peter said 'You certainly know the finer points of life'.

Julian replied 'I was not brought up to it but I enjoy the things money can by. I also like good music and if I have an indulgence it is to provide the right ambience for the mood I am trying to create.

Tonight we are just relaxing so we can pick up our lobster claws in our hands and enjoy the food. Tony knows what to provide. If we were entertaining girls they worry about sticky fingers and splashing their clothes so for them we would provide, say, swordfish steaks and use knives and forks!

Tony will ask you if you enjoyed the salad dressing so please ensure you try it. You will not be disappointed'. There was fruit where you would expect to see vegetables, all beautifully displayed, and unobtrusive helpings of caviar on toast. 'Have a soldier' said Julian.

They took their time over the meal and Julian said 'We don't go for dessert much but please say if you would like one'. Peter said he was of the same taste.

Tony reappeared with a coffee tray and the Spanish girl was ready to clear the table.

They moved to one of the cream leather sofas and Julian said 'Break out that Champagne Cognac we picked up in Marseilles'. Tony poured the precious amber liquid into crystal balloon glasses. 'Well' exclaimed Julian 'Do you want to live like me - do you want a job?'

So, Peter considered, I have been softened up for the job. 'Tell me about the terms' he replied.

Julian said 'I will pay you £10,000 a month out of which you can sort out your

own tax if you feel you must. I will provide the cash for trips to Blighty, say every couple of weeks, but you are on call
to me at all times. You will stay with us
on the boat or at the villa. I will provide a
car and you can return that truck you like
so much. In return I need your absolute
discretion and trust and you may be called
upon to assist in business transactions not
connected to construction'.

Such as?' asked Peter.

'You are either in or out' replied Julian. 'Your contract is for as long as it suits
me but you cannot quit without my agree-
ment. I pay for everything with cash and
before you ask that is because I cannot get
rid of it any other way'.

'You're on' said Peter.

While these negotiations were going
on Danny had cruised the yacht in a big
circle and Marbella was not far off. Julian
and Peter returned to the bridge. Julian
said 'OK Danny, I will bring her in'. They
entered the harbour and Julian expertly
turned the yacht about and berthed her
without any fuss.

Peter realised how tired he was and
requested he retire to his cabin. He lay
on his bed and wondered what he had let

himself in for. He slept late and joined the others for an English breakfast.

CHAPTER 14

Julian said, 'Peter I want you to go and buy some new clothes, including a couple of suits. Here, take my car and go into Marbella town. You have some cash I believe' referring to the £5,000 Peter had been given back home, he presumed.

The car was a red Porsche 911 convertible and Peter realised another dream as he sped along the highway to the boutiques. I am trusted out alone today he thought.

In the shops the assistants' spoke English and he chose clothes similar in style to his new found friends. He drove back to the parked Nissan, which was now looking dustier than ever. After some deliberation he moved it into a side street. He gathered his belongings that he thought he might need and put them in the Porsche.

On returning to the yacht he said to Julian 'I called the hire company and asked them to collect the Nissan from the car park. I left the keys with the attendant'.

In the next few days Julian and Peter visited the two villas that Julian owned and a newly completed golf course up in the hills towards Manuel's farm. Peter was introduced to the golf club set and was impressed by the high esteem in which Julian held.

Julian showed Peter potential building land at the edge of the golf course. He said 'Why don't you sketch what you would like to see built there. The local architects will be best at house design but they will welcome your input on layout and landscaping'. 'But I am not an architect I am a builder and developer'. Julian carried on unheeded.

'There is an architect's office on site and I suggest you borrow a computer or whatever you need and work here for a few days. You can stay at the golf club. I have some business to do here so see you later'.

Peter acquainted himself with the architects; apparently it was common practice to share facilities. He was able to get a detailed plan of the area for building on to the computer screen and proceeded to plan a small village of select villas with a communal swimming pool theme. He was delighted to be working again and the architect willingly helped him, making sure the drawing was coloured properly showing lots of trees that would impress Julian.

During the first day he made his phone calls. The hospital said it appeared that Jane had moved her position slightly in bed although tests showed she was no nearer consciousness. He felt a faint hope of improvement, but would she be her old self?

He called the school and the Headmaster said exams were over and both boys were fine. Was it OK for them to go on a school trip camping in the Brecon Beacons with a teacher and other boys? After all he had spent many hours there in training himself. So Peter agreed. He also rang his sports club and spoke to a friend who worked there. He asked him to visit his house and check that everything was secure.

He told the friend where to find the spare key to the front door and asked him to check the mail and pay any bills. He arranged for some money to be sent to his friend's bank. His own Bank Manager said on the phone 'I suppose you want this arranged without your signature'. 'Yes please, is my word good enough?' 'It is' the Manager replied.

On the third afternoon at the golf club complex Julian reappeared. He said 'It occurs to me I left you stranded here without a car. You should have said'. Peter replied that all he needed was on site and he had even bought some clothes and toiletries from the golf club shop.

He showed Julian his work to date and Julian was genuinely impressed. He said

'Don't worry; once we agree the general layout the locals can implement construction.

Never get involved in detail, that's my motto'.

Peter observed, it might be Julian's motto on construction but on board the yacht Julian checked every detail. This led Peter to believe that whatever part the yacht played in generating money, it was the major part.

Julian said 'That's enough work for a while, let the architects take it on to the next stage. You and I will return to the yacht'. They motored down through the hills with the sun still hot in the open top Porsche.

CHAPTER 15

Julian said 'It's time to put to sea; we have work to do and a long way to go. Why not freshen up and I will see you on the bridge'.

By the time Peter reached the bridge Julian was in his seat, drink in hand and resplendent in his nautical kit as he called it.

Peter said 'Where are we going?'

Julian replied 'Down the coast past Estapona, La Linen, to the Tauta Point across the Straits of Gibraltar to Tangier. How does that sound?'

'Sounds fine, how long will it take?'

'Well it's a little under a hundred miles, so allow four or five hours.'

We have some goods to pick up'. He started the engines, cast off and repeated the delicate manoeuvre out of the harbour.

They cruised down the coast but this time there was an air of purpose on board and no one spoke much. Julian let Peter take the helm and showed him how to follow the compass and landmarks to remain on course.

The girl brought coffee to the bridge and no more alcohol was offered. It was a warm evening but the cloud was covering the moon. They were making nearly 15 knots when Peter noticed they were not showing navigation lights let alone the party lights.

He said 'Have you forgotten the lights Julian?'

'No' said Julian and did not elaborate.

On and on they sailed until Julian said 'There is Tanta and now we turn to port across the Straits. Anyone following us will show on radar and Danny is checking that on a monitor below decks'.

'Why the secrecy?' asked Peter. Julian looked annoyed and said 'We are collecting drugs, as if you didn't know. Stop this naïve attitude. I am not fooled and you had plenty of time to walk away. You are in now, and if we were caught tonight, you would rot in jail with the rest of us!'

Peter watched Julian's face and thought; I must not rile him again. God knows what he might do if he snaps. Peter had no fear of his fellow man and usually his appearance and the respect he seemed to command, without trying, meant people did not trifle with him. He also knew Julian could summon his men, probably armed.

Julian regained his composure in seconds and said 'Mind you if they do stop us I promise you they won't find anything, so relax'.

CHAPTER 16

Off the cost of Tangier they hove to, waited with engines ticking over to maintain position. Soon a motor launch appeared alongside with muffled engines and no lights.

Julian said 'You might find it interesting to join the boys on the starboard side'. Peter left the bridge and did as suggested.

Just in time he saw a smooth streamlined object about six feet long being winched aboard with the help of a small electric davit.

In the gloom it looked like a shark with dorsal fin and keel fin. Someone had even painted an evil eye on the front end. It hung by two wires attached to hooks on the casing. It was lowered onto the deck of the yacht and Tony lifted the quick release panel and placed plastic packets into the compartment as they transferred them from the launch.

Nodding, he passed four plastic boxes as payment to the launch skipper. The launch crept away into the night and not a word was spoken.

Peter spoke and Tony almost leapt out of his skin exclaiming 'I wish you wouldn't do that!'

'The crew are confined to their quarters in case someone nicks our idea or spills the beans somewhere. I thought I was alone. Anyway let me explain. This is a paravane and is ballasted to travel beneath the water. Think of it as a remote control submarine.'

'Obviously it cannot keep up with us so what we do is let it trail behind the boat on a stainless steel wire. It has an electric motor so if we are approached it can make way at about 4 knots. We can choose perhaps to send it deep or run it under our keel.'

'Customs boats circle suspect craft to ensure there are no drug hauls beneath the water in fishing nets for example, but they can't deal with this moving target. Their sonar can't detect it if it's under our keel. Also, although we have never had to use it, we can release it from the line if they spot it. You can't go to jail for losing your fishing tackle. The line is run round from the stern to the hook on the nose so all we do now is lower it gently into the water and as soon as we get under way it falls astern. I return below and monitor its progress on our own radar'.

Peter asked 'What happens when we come into berth?'

'That's simple. We come in very slowly and the Paravane is running just below our keel. We moor up and leave it there overnight in case we get any visitors on arrival or if we are being watched.

The following night a speedboat comes alongside for drinks and the paravane line is transferred to the stern of the speedboat. When it leaves harbour the paravane is trailing only about ten feet behind but the wash from the speedboat masks it. The paravane is taken across the bay to a quiet landing place and only Julian knows what happens then'.

As Paradise gathered speed the paravane duly fell behind and Tony returned to his cabin to monitor progress. Peter returned to the bridge and Julian, looking cool as ever, said 'Well what do you think of my expensive fish?'

Peter duly praised the idea and thought what a clever way of transporting misery and death to the weak.

Peter said 'Forgive me; I do not know much about drugs, what is it?

'That is pure heroin and worth about half a million pounds on the streets, but don't forget we have expenses out of that'.

They cruised back up the coast at a leisurely 12 knots and did not see another vessel. At the approach to the harbour mouth of Pureto Banus they slowed right down and Peter knew that Tony would be guiding the paravane beneath the keel.

Julian carried out his expert turn and crept quietly stern first into their mooring. Peter felt an eerie sensation at the thought of the paravane settling against the hull of Paradise. When the yacht was secured the four men gathered for a drink in the Stateroom. They were quiet at first, as the job could not be considered complete until they had off loaded the following night.

Peter asked 'How often do you make this run?'

Julian replied 'About once a week but obviously we vary the times and watch the weather forecasts'.

Peter calculated, that means, even allowing for generous expenses, a cargo worth £250,000 a week. Then he realised he did not know how much heroin cost in Tangier. Still it meant enormous profits. They each retired to their quarters.

CHAPTER 17

Peter tried to summarise events. A man crashed a car into his wife's car, they swap drivers. This man offers a free trip to Spain to cheer Peter up; Peter makes friends with a local whom he feels he can rely on to support him. He becomes the employee of a drug runner and wonders if Julian had already researched his profession and was satisfied that he could legitimately use Peter to expand the construction side. After all, even in Spain someone may want to know how Julian lives so well.

He thought; if I inform the Police they are probably already in the know and turn a blind eye for cash and favours.

If I do, Julian will know and I would need to leave the country very quickly. He realised now that Julian was utterly ruthless and although he would never be seen to get his hands dirty, there were plenty of thugs for hire in Spain. A phone call would be all that's needed for Peter to disappear. What would be more interesting would be to find out what happens to the heroin when it gets to Malaga. The idea of tracking the source in Tangier was a nonstarter as drugs were rife and he would be out of his depth where life is cheap. 'Anyway all I want is Julian'.

He resolved to find out as much as he could about Julian and his affairs. He knew that next day he must stay at Julian's disposal and no doubt would be watched for he could not believe that Julian totally trusted anyone.

They breakfasted late and Julian said 'I would like you to come to the new villa this afternoon. I think it may be better to keep attention away from the yacht and we can set up communications from there. We will take the Porsche, you can drive; it is in El Hauvin le Grande. Please study the map as I have an aversion to giving directions. Don't forget to bring some clothes'.

Peter did as requested and also noted that if Puerto Banus was the base, then El Hauvin le Grande and the area where Manuel's farm was, formed a triangle upside down. That meant if he needed Manuel in a hurry he could cut across country.

Although heaven knows what the roads
were like.

CHAPTER 18

Early in the afternoon the two of them set off to the new villa. Julian dozed most of the way but Peter enjoyed the little red super car, and the breeze was a welcome relief from the heat.

It was a winding black tarmac road and the scenery was the parched brown scrubland that characterises that part of inland Spain. Just over an hour passed and they approached El Hauvin le Grande. It was siesta time; the older buildings were shuttered and all was quiet. Julian became alert and directed Peter off left up a hill into an expensive residential area. All the villas were screened from the road by tall hedges, which bore brilliant flowers. Big black gates were the order of the day.

Julian directed Peter to one villa set apart from the others. He pointed a zapper at the security panel and the gates swung open. Up a short drive with immaculate gardens they approached the pillared front door. Julian leaned over and pressed the horn of the car. The sturdy front door opened and a young Spanish girl appeared in housemaid uniform, including a little white apron.

They walked into the house that was cool and dark, shuttered from the sun. He asked the girl in poor Spanish to open the shutters and said bashfully 'Peter I am actually afraid of the dark'. Peter logged the information in his memory.

The house was furnished and decorated in the Moors style with marble floors, heavy baroque furniture and huge vases everywhere.

Julian said 'I don't know if you like the decoration but I bought the place furnished'. They walked through the living room and opened the patio doors onto the terrace. A swimming pool was immaculately displayed before them. 'Would you like a drink Peter? Chilled Champagne perhaps?'

Peter nodded. The housemaid was hovering discreetly. She understood sufficient English and withdrew.

They settled at the poolside table and swinging sofa. The swimming pool looked inviting and the view from the terrace looked down the valley to the sea. Champagne arrived in an ice bucket with a little dish of green olives.

Peter said 'You live a charmed existence, Julian'.

Julian replied 'The risks are high but I like the excitement and I am gradually setting funds aside to have legitimate businesses'.

Suddenly switching the subject he said 'Were you happily married? Or should I have said, are you? Before you answer you have not requested "home leave" as it were. No doubt you have telephoned the hospital - I suppose there is no change? What about your boys - don't you miss them? Can you phone them? Would you like to visit the UK? Shortly? How far would you like to go with me?'

Danny and Tony are very good at what they do on board but they are not businessmen. I notice that you have a commercial mind. If I knew your aspirations we could talk about a right hand man role'.

Peter spoke as Julian paused, saying 'You have just asked a lot of questions without waiting for answers. What is happily married? It is difficult to answer with my temperament, where I have a family, for whom I would do anything but unable to show it. As things are now I feel that my wife will not recover from her coma and even if she does, she will be severely disabled.

'With boarding school the boys will become independent and probably go on to university. So I feel life can never be the same'.

Privately to himself, he prayed that Jane would make a full recovery and that his boys would always be close to him even if none of them would admit it.

'So you see Julian, I recognise I am at a crossroads in my life. That is as accurate as I can be right now. However, I was going to ask you if I could go home soon. What do you think?'

Julian swirled an olive on a stick in the champagne. 'It's important that you visit your family. I don't have one and I envy you. England is only a couple of hours away so it is no problem. Do your boys like cars?'

'Yes' said Peter, puzzled.

'Would you take the Porsche back home for me? I have a flat in the Bathwick area of Bath, with Mews garages, and I would like to base the car there. I know I could buy a car in Bath but I try not to conduct any business there as Bath is like a small village and word travels. You can put the car on the train if you wish or drive it over. I recommend you drive up the French coast and make it a motoring holiday. If you like, take your boys around Devon or somewhere for a few days'.

Peter said. 'It's half term this coming weekend, is that too soon?'

'Its only Tuesday' replied Julian. 'While you are away think about what I have said.'

'I know your wife's health will decide matters but you only live once'.

They talked on as the sun went down slowly. It was agreed that Peter would take the Porsche and head for a channel crossing on Friday.

Julian said he had a few phone calls to make 'Why don't you have a swim?'

'I don't have any shorts' replied Peter.

'There is no one but the maid to see you' laughed Julian 'and she is busy in the house. There is a towel in your bedroom, let me show you your room'.

CHAPTER 19

Peter was left to his own devices. He stripped and wrapped the towel round his waist and padded barefoot down to the terrace. Embarrassed, he removed the towel and dived into the sparkling water. He was a strong swimmer and churned the water to foam as he surged up and down the pool.

He counted twenty lengths of the pool and pulled himself onto the patio feeling refreshed and invigorated. Before he could reach for the towel the maid appeared and walked towards him with his glass of champagne. Sheepishly he accepted the drink; the girl's eyes did not leave his face. She turned and walked away. Suddenly there was a loud laugh from an upstairs window. Julian, telephone in hand, had set him up and timed it to perfection.

'Get some clothes on and let's go out on the town. Do you like flamenco dancing?'

Peter dried himself and returned to the bedroom. He drew back the heavy curtains and took in the view. Lights were beginning to twinkle as dusk fell.

Julian called out 'Put on one of your floral shirts and jeans and I will do the same'. He even tells me what to wear, thought Peter.

Julian drove into El Havrin le Grande and parked outside a restaurant called 'Alcotain'.

He said 'The place is painted white inside and out - the colour is in the food'.

They walked into the little reception area where a short overweight Spaniard clapped his hands and exclaimed 'Senor Wilding - a pleasure to see you as always'. Julian beamed at the recognition. 'Hello Pablo' he said. They were led through a little passage into a courtyard with tables around it.

The place was half full already, a mixture of locals and tourists, but no children, Peter noticed.

Wicker chairs were pulled out for them and Pablo spread red gingham check napkins on their laps. A waiter arrived with a carafe of chilled white wine and glasses.

Pablo said to Peter 'Here are the menus but I must tell you what is special tonight. I recommend the Rodaballo, Mr Wilding knows the dish. It is a big favourite in Andalusia'.

Julian said, 'If you like fish you will love this. It is turbot baked with garlic, parsley, bay leaves and white wine'.

Peter liked the sound of this and nodded his approval. Julian took over and ordered Gaspacho, the cold garlic laden tomato soup with croutons to start.

He chose a wine from his own memory called Marques de Alella. '82 was a good year Pablo, if you have it'. Pablo congratulated them on their choice and withdrew.

The Gaspacho was served instantly with rough bread. Peter said 'I never feel anything but amazed at your knowledge of food and drink'. Julian replied 'You mentioned that before on the evening of our first meal aboard Paradise'.

Not only did he remember the remark, he also remembered where and when he said it, thought Peter. He does not miss a trick.

The wine arrived and Julian tasted the pale, distinctive tasting, wine. 'So you did have the 1982 Pablo'. 'Si Senor'.

He leaned over to Peter and whispered 'I was bluffing but Pablo agrees with his customers, always'.

This harmless sense of fun endeared Peter to the drug running villain who had injured his wife so badly, and had bought his sense of decency as well. 'That is what I must allow Julian to think anyway'.

The Rodaballo arrived, steaming hot and they engrossed themselves in their food. Peter wiped his bread in the sauce with his fork. Julian said 'You like Rodaballo, I can see'.

Dessert was not offered but the cheese plate arrived with the three Mancheyo cheeses.

Julian informed him that there were more than 500 cheeses made in Spain, and these were from the local region. 'Make sure you try each one. Now let's sit back for the flamenco'.

CHAPTER 20

In a few minutes a guitarist and violinist appeared and struck up a tune, encouraging people to clap. The tempo quickened and the artistes came dancing into the courtyard.

The girl in a scarlet silk dress had long black hair that shone and flowed as she moved. With white flowers in her hair and ebony castanets in her hands, she clattered and stamped towards her partner.

The man in toreador pants, white frilly shirt open to the navel, and high black heels, snapped his castanets and stamped his feet to the music. Swaying to and fro, they circled each other in the gypsy dance of their ancestors.

The tempo increased and the staccato of the castanets responded like machine gun fire.

Whirling and swaying ever faster, their bodies began to shine with sweat. Stamping even louder the girl plucked the flowers from her hair and threw them to the men in the audience. The diners were on their feet, clapping and stamping to the beat as the crescendo approached.

The male danced closer, his leg muscles straining against the tight black pants. Sweating profusely, his white shirt was wet and body hair was showing through.

The two dancers circled for the last time, faced each other for a moment in the final movement of ritual courtship, stamping and clattering in a cacophony of noise. Then the male dancer scythed his arm through the air in a cutting motion. Dancers, musicians and spectators stopped abruptly and the silence was deafening.

The dancers stood motionless for a moment as the applause began and for the first time smiled their appreciation.

Pablo appeared and put a shawl around the girl's shoulders and kissed her hand.

The diners resumed their meals and wine drinking, although they were strangely quiet. The dancers slipped quietly away.

CHAPTER 21

Julian said 'I find the flamenco lends an erotic feel to the evening. Better than the peculiar bopping and shaking we Brits were weaned on'.

Peter came down to earth at this great leveller of a conversationalist, sitting next to him.

'I thought we would discuss the arrangements for your trip but I am not in the mood now. It can wait until tomorrow'.

They sat and chatted about life in Spain and money and the toys it can buy.

Julian said 'I am thinking of buying a Ferrari to pull the birds but I suppose a Mercedes limmo would fit the business image better. What do you think?'

'An agonising choice' said Peter laconically.

They both laughed.

'Let's hit the hay' said Julian and stood up. He walked towards Pablo with Peter catching him up. He thrust a handful of

Euro notes into Pablo's hand and they both thanked him for their evening.

Julian drove back to the villa himself. They were both quiet and went straight to their rooms.

Peter lay naked on his bed for a while thinking about his return to reality at the weekend.

Sleep overtook him and the next thing he knew was the maid offering him a cup of coffee in the morning. In poor English she said 'Please join Mr Wilding on the patio for breakfast'.

'Morning Peter. I trust you slept well?'

'All night' replied Peter truthfully.

They ate a light continental breakfast.

Meanwhile, Julian rattled off instructions in a business like manner. He said 'I will drop you off at the Marina this morning and you can pick up the jeep that Danny and Tony drive around in. Go up to the new development and check the progress. The architects should have things ready to start construction. Bring their drawings to me with your comments. I want start dates and building cost estimates. If they can't produce estimates tell them we will withhold their fees until they can produce the information. That usually speeds things up.'

'I expect you will want to pop across to that peasant farmer friend you have, although God knows what you two have in common. Make your own arrangements for your drive up to the channel crossing. In case I forget to mention it ask customs to stamp your passport. They don't bother much these days with the EU and all that. If the Inland Revenue become interested in you later you can prove legitimate travel and expenses. We will meet here Thursday afternoon. Pick up the Porsche and enjoy your break'.

Peter did his errands and made out a report of the progress on the new development. He was surprised how well the team had progressed without supervision. He concluded they were paid well and wanted it to last.

He drove down to the Marina and collected some travelling clothes. Danny and Tony were aboard Paradise. Tony said 'I hear you are on the payroll now. He's a good boss - don't abuse it'.

Peter replied 'I have been fortunate to find a chance like this to make some money'.

Relay that message he thought.

He drove back to the villa on Wednesday afternoon and telephoned the hospital.

The nurse said, 'No change but no deterioration'.

He phoned the school. The boys were in class but the housemaster said that he was pleased with their progress in school. Peter said 'I will be home in time for half term to pick them up'. The housemaster said they would be pleased and he would ensure they were ready.

He studied the maps and calculated his stopping places en route. Knowing himself well he knew he would drive eight or nine hours at a time, stopping only for fuel and food. The idea of the Porsche in his custody filled him with anticipation.

He walked down to the pool feeling overdressed in his swim shorts and wristwatch.

He swam, leisurely this time, until the ever attentive maid showed up and offered to cook an omelette for him. She produced English newspapers only one day old. He tried to engage her in conversation but her servile upbringing forbade fraternisation.

All the same, he thought, she is a gem and she has seen me without my shorts on.

He fantasised but she kept her distance. Evidently more afraid of Julian than of him.

Nothing for it but an early night and wait for Julian.

After a lazy breakfast, Julian appeared and he reported in detail the progress at the new development. Julian seemed satisfied. He said 'The Porsche is fuelled up and clean. I have put some of my personal gear in it. Please put it in the flat. My sports bag and squash rackets are there. I will make a point of playing when in Bath. It's too hot over here.'

'These are the keys to the flat and the address is on the label. The mews garage is at the back of the building, just drive through the arch. You can leave the Porsche keys on the hall table'. Peter put his luggage in the front of the Porsche.

'That's it, I'm ready' said Peter.

'Not quite' Julian replied and produced two red toy Porsches, each about the size of a shoebox. 'Tell the boys to put those on display in their bedrooms. Don't forget to come back to Spain or I shall have to come and collect you. When you return, ring here at the villa and someone will collect you from the airport'.

Julian walked back into the villa leaving Peter to gaze at the two model cars. He jumped into the car, put his folded map on the passenger seat and drove off.

CHAPTER 22

Following the main autoroutes he reckoned to be in the Saragossa region by early morning.

The Porsche was a joy to drive and he ate up the miles, passing through quiet towns and villages. With the fuel gauge down to a quarter tank full he would fill up, stretch his legs and have a cold drink. The petrol stations seemed more modern than any of the other buildings.

As early evening approached, he drove into the little town of Borja and looked for a hotel. He chose a small clean looking building, set back from the road. The receptionist was reserved but polite. She showed him to a small cool room and suggested he dine at 9pm when it was cooler. He showered and changed and had time for a stroll.

Walking out of the front door of the hotel he looked fondly at the now dusty Porsche with squashed insects all over the front.

He chose a Bodega for a drink and sampled the local wine, trying to memorise the name to impress Julian. The town was sleepy and quiet and Peter wondered how the Spanish spent their time. Watching TV, he concluded. It's the same the world over he thought sadly.

Returning to the hotel, he went straight to the dining room. The only other diners were the hotel owner's family.

He accepted the suggestion to try the Boqerones, not knowing what it was. A small plate of whole little fish similar to sardines arrived. They were arranged in a fantail, and his hosts were eating them whole by picking them up and dropping them into their mouths by the tail. He did the same.

They asked him if he was enjoying Spain and where he was heading. Their natural reserve suited Peter, as he did not want to answer too many questions.

The main course arrived. To Peter it was a tasty casserole and he finished every morsel. He asked what it was 'Rabo do toro a la rondene' they said. Peter turned the words over in his mind. He gave up. The receptionist who had greeted him said 'stewed bulls tail to you'. Everyone laughed.

This time dessert was put on the table. There were Pestions or honey-coated pancakes.

As soon as coffee was finished Peter thanked them for their company and retired to his room.

He studied his map and reckoned he was about 100 miles from the French border. Although he would lose time through the Pyrenees, he looked forward to the scenery.

He decided that if he applied himself and got an early start he would drive up through the Bordeaux & Loire districts and be North West of Paris by evening. This, he guessed, was 400 miles. He rang the hotel reception and asked if they would provide a packed lunch.

He went to bed and began to think about his family and the life he used to lead. Sleep overtook his thoughts and he woke at first light, refreshed and ready to go.

After a quick coffee with his hosts, he was on the road again and soon climbing into the Pyrenees Mountains. He crossed the border with the minimum of formalities and started the long haul up through the famous vineyards. He would have been delighted to stop for a tasting session but it would hinder his progress.

Perhaps he would return one day. 'With whom?' he wondered. A disabled wife, a girlfriend, even Julian the wine buff. One thing is for sure; you need to share pleasant times.

At midday he stopped just long enough to eat his packed lunch of cold chicken, tomatoes and bread. There was a can of Coke in the bag as well. Not the most enjoyable meal, he thought, but it will keep me going.

On he drove and as teatime approached he deliberately stayed well west of Paris and all the traffic. A quick look at the map and he decided to get past Rouen and call it a day.

He reached Gourney and began to look for a hotel. A clean efficient looking pension presented itself and he pulled in. Yes they could accommodate him. He walked stiffly back to the car for his overnight bag. He realised his eyes were sore from the driving and a slight headache had descended upon him from the prolonged period of concentration.

He checked into his room and collapsed wearily on to the bed. Unintentionally he fell asleep for about an hour. Feeling better he pondered over the wisdom of such a long drive. Did Julian appreciate how far it was? It was a lovely car to drive but maybe you can have too much of a good thing.

He decided that a shower, followed hopefully by a good French meal would restore him.

After the shower and fresh clothes, he felt ready for the restaurant. He was pleased that the diners were eating early and he sat at the bar and studied the menu. In spite of the tempting local specialities he chose onion soup, followed by a steak in garlic butter. He asked for a glass of the house red and the bar attendant laughed and said, 'We have dozens of reds for you to try'. Peter soon relaxed in the company of the locals and it occurred to him that he was becoming something of an authority on food and wine. He wondered if his friends back home would notice a change in him.

He enjoyed his evening and learnt a little French, realising that he could make friends more easily in France and Spain than in England where the chances were he would have dined alone in silence. He retired to bed, feeling much happier.

'Tomorrow morning, on up to Calais and a quick drive home to Bath'. He thought.

Another early start and he joined the next available ferry. With his car safely stowed on board he strolled on deck beneath grey skies and feeling the cold.

CHAPTER 23

The ferry docked at Dover and he drove the car into the customs lane. He chose the green channel and the Customs Officer stopped him and asked him to open him his luggage. He asked the statutory question 'Did you pack these bags?' Julian said yes, except the sports bag that belonged to a friend.

The officer said 'As you are bringing it into the country, it is your responsibility'

He looked long and hard at Peter and unzipped the bag. Removing the contents he felt around inside the bag. Frequently he stared at Peter. Returning his gaze to the contents he settled his attention upon a tin of talcum powder. He shook a little on to his hand. He smelt the powder.

'Oh no' exclaimed Peter aloud, feeling the blood rushing to his face. The officer pressed a button on his desk and another officer joined them. He handed the tin to his associate and looked around the car. 'A very nice car sir. May I see all your

documents? What is your occupation?'
Property Developer said Peter. The officer continued to look in the luggage compartment and glove box. He said 'I notice that you are bringing this car into the UK but you did not take it out'.

'I am taking it to Bath for a friend'.

The second officer returned with the tin of talcum powder and talked quietly to the other officer.

'Just as I thought sir. Its talcum powder' smiled the Customs man. 'Have a safe journey to Bath. I should wash the car when you get there, a dirty Porsche is sacrilege'.

Peter asked his favour 'Could you stamp my passport. I know you don't do it much these days but I like to record my trips'.

The passport was duly stamped and he was free to go. The Customs Officer rubbed his chin thoughtfully as the Porsche disappeared.

Peter made his drivers adjustment to the left side of the road.

Around mid afternoon he arrived in Bath and made straight for the Royal United Hospital. He walked through the corridors thinking about how much had happened since he was last here.

He entered the little room and was horrified to see an empty bed. He stood there, numb. 'Why wasn't I told? My wife died alone while I lived it up in Spain'. He sat in the chair beside the bed with his head in his hands.

'Can I help you sir?' a nurse stood before him.

'I came to see Jane Haynes, I am her husband'.

'Oh she has been moved into the general ward next door to here. Come along, I'll show you'.

Peter, in a daze, followed her into the ward to a bed with screens around it. Jane lay on her back with her head propped on a pillow. Various tubes were connected to her nose and mouth.

Peter said 'Hello Jane' automatically.

'I am afraid she cannot hear you, she has been in a coma for weeks, didn't you know?

'Is there any improvement?' Peter asked.

'She has moved slightly in the bed, which Dr Wylies feels is a very good sign, but that is the only news I can give you. I will leave you together for a while'.

Peter put his hand on his wife's arm and whispered his love for her and realised he could not have spoken to her this way if she was awake. He embarrassed himself.

He left the hospital and drove up to the school hoping to pick up the boys before driving to his house. The housemaster took him to the boys' dormitory. They both leapt up eagerly and he held out his arms. Checking themselves in front of their mates they avoided his gesture and said 'Hello Dad' in unison.

Thomas said 'You look sun tanned. Have you enjoyed camping?'

Changing the subject Peter asked 'Why all the empty beds in here?'

'Its half term Dad, most of the boys have gone home'.

'We thought you had forgotten us'

'It has been a long drive up from Malaga'.

'You drove? The length of Spain and France Dad?' exclaimed Josh.

'All right Josh, don't show off your geography' said Thomas.

'Let's go home boys'.

They walked out to the Porsche. 'I've brought this back for a friend'.

The boys, both keen car fanatics, inspected the car. 'Its very dirty Dad, can we wash it at home please?'

'You don't usually offer to wash the car'.

'Your car is not a Porsche' came the predictable reply.

After an argument about who was to sit in the front, they drove home. The house was silent and smelt as houses do when they are shut up. The mail was piled neatly on the hall table, showing that his friend had been over to check the house.

They opened the windows and turned on some lights. One of the boys played some music.

They all realised something was missing. Jane's bright cheery voice calling out from the kitchen perhaps. The fresh flowers in the vases and fruit on the table. All the little touches that a woman has to make a house a home.

'Nothing in the fridge, of course.'

'Shall we eat out boys?' They all changed their clothes. Peter chose a sedate English sports coat, more in keeping with the climate compared to the short sleeve shirts to which he had become accustomed.

They drove down to the local pub in Freshford village and Peter was reminded that the English pub remains unique in the world. They chose the steak and kidney pie and Peter had his first pint of English beer for some weeks.

As they caught up on each other's news, Peter asked if his sons had managed to get to the hospital. Sheepishly they cast their eyes to the floor. Thomas said 'It's not easy Dad, all we can do is sit and look at mum'.

'That may be true Thomas but remember Mum may be able to hear you even if she cannot show it.'

Peter was dreading the questions on his time spent in Spain and decided to take the initiative.

'I have been very fortunate in being given the chance to run a building development project which includes a housing development, swimming pools, golf course and leisure club'.

'But Dad you don't have the expertise for anything that big'.

'Have faith boys, common sense goes a long way and anyway there are some able people to assist me'.

'How much longer will you be away Dad?'

'A few months but I will come home frequently, so don't worry'.

'Well boys, would you like to go to the coast for a few days in the Porsche?'

Thomas replied matter of factly 'To be honest Dad, we are getting a bit old for a trip to the seaside. It's a nice car but during half term we would just like to see our friends in town. You can drop us off though, so that they can see the car'.

Peter smiled almost sadly. He was losing them as they grew up and like every other parent wished he had given more of his time to them.

They returned to the house and watched TV, although Peter could not stop his mind from wandering.

At 10.30pm Peter called 'Bed time' and after token protests from the boys, they all went upstairs.

Peter undressed and lay in his bed feeling strange without his wife beside him. When in Spain he had not noticed it but the bed felt empty and he felt a longing for his wife.

Guilt overcame him as he realised he had been living it up while his wife lay stricken, and most of all it was the culprit who had encouraged him. How could he hope to teach his boys the evil of drugs when he was on the payroll of a drug dealer? But it was only to get close to Julian while he found a way to bring him to justice, he had reassured himself.

Or was it? He was becoming too involved with Julian and if he was honest he actually liked the man. He forced himself to remember the corruption that Julian dealt in. The bribes, the violence, the misery of drug addiction. But most of all he reminded himself that if Julian had not driven into Jane's car she would be lying in bed with him now. The truth leapt to the front of his mind. Julian did not give a damn about the state Jane was in.

He drifted off to sleep and in the morning decided he should drive to the airport and collect his own car, left there some weeks ago, when he flew to Spain.

CHAPTER 24

He got up early and went to the local shop and bought eggs, bacon, tomatoes and bread to make a big breakfast for the three of them.

Reluctantly the boys left their beds but were impressed by his new found cooking skills. He explained the need to collect his car but they chose not to go with him.

He rang his long-standing pal Chris, and asked him if he would drive him to Bristol Airport. He knew he would be teased about the Porsche.

Chris turned up at the house and said 'Won the pools have you?'

Peter said 'It's not mine, but you can drive it to the airport'.

This side tracked his friend completely as he took the wheel. Peter found out the hard way that long term parking at airports was expensive.

Chris said he doubted Peter's car would start after being left and it would be cheaper to just leave the car there.

However, start it did and Chris noticed that Peter paid the parking fee from a big wad of £20 notes. Normally Peter used his credit card or more likely borrowed from Chris when they were out. Peter usually had enough money to live as he wanted but was always forgetful about carrying it with him.

Chris said 'Before we drive back separately, let's have a coffee'.

When they were seated in the restaurant he said 'Tell me to mind my own business if you like, but what's going on?' 'Mind your own business' laughed Peter, but explained,

'We have been friends for a very long time and there is something going on. It may well be that I will need your help over the next few weeks. I am afraid to say too much now, please understand'.

Chris said 'Pick up the phone when you need me'. His friendship gave Peter a warm feeling as they drove the cars back to Bath.

They shook hands rather formally as Chris got back into his own car.

During the afternoon the boys, as good as their word, washed the Porsche amid clouds of soapsuds and buckets of water being thrown at one another. Peter enjoyed the lighthearted play of his sons and thanked them for their efforts.

'Pocket money would be more useful' said Thomas. Peter paid his dues with a £10 note each. Behind his back Josh said 'I reckon dad's come into some money'.

The telephone rang later and they were invited to supper at Jane's parents. Glad to avoid having to try to cook, Peter drove the boys round in his own car. He was beginning to tire of the interest in the Porsche.

They spent a long time discussing the practicalities of Peter working abroad and the future if Jane did not recover. Peter did not want the children upset and just assured them it would all turn out all right. Feeling oppressed, he made his excuses and they returned home.

The next day he drove down to Julian's flat in Henrietta Street and let himself in. The flat was tastefully furnished and he remembered Julian bought it complete with furniture. Although it was comfortable it did not have any of the clutter that shows a house is lived in, and none of Julian's personal belongings were to be seen. Peter concluded that Julian had not owned it for very long. He made a mental note to find out how Julian had bought it. Surely the taxman would be interested.

'Although I have bigger fish to fry than that'.

He went out of the flat and walked around the back through the arch as directed. Two rows of six garages faced each other in a courtyard and he chose his garage by the number on the key ring.

Opening the doors he wondered if there would be any of the usual rubbish everyone accumulates. Maybe even drugs stashed away, he laughed quietly to himself. The garage was completely empty and clean.

He brought the Porsche around from the road and drove it into the garage. He wondered how long it would be before Julian came over to stay. It seemed a pity to leave the car there.

Surprised at his own extravagance he took a taxi back to his house. Something played on his mind for the rest of the day. Yes, this was out of character for Julian to just dump an expensive toy and not use it. Like all businessmen he did not like to waste money.

Julian had a good reason for everything he did but Peter could not see the logic of this. He did not seem to go to the U.K. much and had not mentioned the Range Rover that was involved in the accident. So that was two cars in Bath now.

CHAPTER 25

All evening he sat in his chair with a drink, feeling more and more uneasy. He went to bed and this time could not sleep. He looked at the clock a dozen times.

At about One a.m, his thoughts began to focus as he went back over his entry through customs. His heart began to pound as the possibilities dawned on him.

He picked up the telephone and rang Chris who lived alone. 'Chris did you ever see the film The French Connection' with Gene Hackman?'

Chris chuckled sleepily and asked if it was vital that Peter had to ask his opinion on films at one o'clock in the morning.

'You are lucky I am home this early'.

'I know it's a lot to ask but would you come round to my house and bring that smart tool kit you've got'.

Chris, always glad of a bit of excitement said 'Tell me more'.

'Not on the phone - see you soon'.

When Chris arrived Peter had the coffee on. He said 'I have a story to tell you' and poured out the events to date.

Chris did not interrupt but absorbed the details.

'Peter, forgive me, but where does Gene Hackman fit into this?'

'Do you remember how they suspected a car was carrying drugs and stripped it down and found a huge cache of drugs hidden in the chassis? Well it's possible that's what I have brought into the country. What do you think?'

Chris replied 'So now you want me to give up my night's sleep and strip that Porsche to bits'.

'Well?' asked Peter.

'Let's go'.

They crept quietly out of the house and took Chris's Range Rover complete with the toolbox. The roads were deserted and Peter dreaded a policeman stopping them for a routine check. What would they say?

They drove quietly to Henrietta Street and around to the mews garage.

'Leave the car in the road. It will look suspicious outside of the garage'. Peter slid the key into the garage door lock. The

129

moonlight was enough for him to spot the light switch on the wall.

'Close the door behind you Chris. If anyone sees a light they will think it was left on accidentally'.

'Well Chris what do you know about the construction of Porsches?'

They both went down on hands and knees and looked under the car and in the front luggage compartment. They looked for signs of recent panel removal.

'How much do we dare strip down? The professional traffickers even put false bottoms in fuel tanks, we will never figure that out'.

'Let's start systematically from the front'. Suggested Chris. They tapped and probed to no avail.

Peter said 'What is this plastic panel behind the front wheels for?'

'Where?'

'Here up under the wing'.

'That's just to keep the mud from collecting in the cavity'.

'Well there you are then'.

'Does every sentence you utter begin with the word well'?

They laughed together as they shared the banter accumulated over many years.

They jacked up the front of the car and removed the road wheel. A ring of small screws held the plastic panel in position. Carefully they pulled the panel away.

Packed tightly in the cavity were plastic packs of white powder!

'Don't touch it' said Chris 'We may not be able to pack it back in. How much is it worth do you think?'

'I don't know, but the stuff may be packed away in other parts of the car too.'

'We had better put the car back together quickly. If someone comes snooping around we are in trouble'. Within minutes the car was back on the ground.

'We need a plan from here' said Chris. 'You are OK because it's doubtful Customs recorded you coming in. They didn't stamp your passport did they?

'Well yes they did' said Peter.

Chris said 'You've been set up I'm afraid. What this Julian has done is take out insurance by ensuring your passport was stamped. If you go to the Police he will deny even knowing you. You have imported a car full of drugs Peter. You should not have gotten into this'.

'Let's go back to the house'. They drove back in silence.

Peter entered the house first and checked the boys were still asleep. The two friends sat at the kitchen table.

Chris said 'The first thing is to decide if you can handle this or just go to the Police and hope they believe you'.

'But I can contribute so much to breaking this whole thing up and ensure Julian is caught. Otherwise he's smart enough to avoid capture'.

'Be honest Peter, you have a vendetta against this man. Don't get carried away'.

'Wait a minute, maybe the matter resolves itself. Our Police do not have any authority in Spain anyway'.

Gradually they hatched a plan. Chris thanked Peter for an interesting night and went home to salvage what was left of a night's sleep.

CHAPTER 26

At first light Peter called the Bath Police station and asked for PC Enfield. He was due in later in the morning and Peter left a message for him to contact him.

When the phone rang PC Enfield sounded somewhat exasperated. He said 'I think I had better come to see you'.

A rather stern PC Enfield arrived. He informed Peter that the Police were a little concerned about Peter's interference, especially posing as a Police officer. He said 'Quite honestly I had to protect you by saying you were just over reacting to your wife's injuries'.

'I don't remember posing as a Police officer'.

'We had an official complaint from a Mr Barnes' solicitor who says you harassed him. We said we would investigate but we were puzzled because the solicitor turned out to be from an expensive London firm. Talk about a sledgehammer to crack a walnut. It took us sometime to realise that it was not one of our officers. Frankly the solicitor is sceptical. What is going on Mr Haynes?'

Peter said 'I will tell you but promise you won't arrest me half way through!' He explained how he deduced that Barney was not the driver of the car on the night of the crash. He explained how he tricked Barney into admitting it.

'That's easy, Mr Haynes, we will issue a warrant for the arrest of his passenger. Do you know who it is?'

'Yes I do and he lives in Spain'.

'That's the end of that then. Sorry Mr Haynes, we cannot extradite him from Spain'.

'I haven't finished yet' Peter said.

He proceeded to fill in sufficient detail for PC Enfield to take the bait.

'I shall have to refer this matter to my superiors Mr Haynes. I am taking you down to the station and will arrange for a senior officer of the drugs squad to be there'.

He set up the meeting by phone and they drove down to the Police Station.

A grim faced Police Superintendent was introduced as Supt. Reynolds. He listened to the story and said 'Mr Haynes, you are in it up to the neck'.

Peter, refusing to be panicked explained that with his help they could arrest the people who would be distributing the drugs.

'I am not sure we need an amateur's help'.

PC Enfield spoke up 'Do you have a plan?'

Supt. Reynolds looked bored.

Peter suggested they put an electronic monitor on the Porsche and track it when the driver collects it. That way Julian would not be alerted.

Supt. Reynolds said 'At this point we take over. I want you to go home Mr Haynes, talk to no one. You do not know the kind of people you are dealing with. PC Enfield, I would like a word'.

As soon as they were alone the Supt. said 'How do you know he is not involved?'

'I think the clue is he did not know this Julian until the car crash. Mr Haynes is an honest clean living family man in my opinion'.

'We shall see Constable, but my team will keep their eye on him. Meanwhile I want you to withdraw your interest in this case and go about your traffic duties'.

'But sir, I wanted to see this through. Peter has been very sensible so far and he deserves some help. After all his wife is in a coma in hospital, all because of this drug pusher'.

The Supt. leaned across the table and spoke in a voice as cold as charity 'The first thing I don't like is someone playing amateur detective; the second thing I don't like is a Constable who questions my orders. I do not spare a second thought for wives in hospital. I intend to smash a drugs ring. Nothing else matters. You may go now PC Enfield'.

The Supt. stared him out of the room.

PC Enfield returned to his patrol car duties feeling sorry for himself. The co-driver was puzzled when he stopped the car at a phone box.

'Mr Hayne's, it's PC Enfield speaking. I have been taken off the case. I have one thing to say to you. You are under suspicion. Think it through but you will not be allowed to participate any further in this country. I trust I have said enough'.

He put the phone down.

Peter was very thoughtful. What message was PC Enfield trying to convey? Got it! "Not in this country" Get back to Spain, ASAP, or the Police will arrest him on suspicion just to keep him from interfering.

He gathered up the boys and apologised, telling them he had to return to Spain immediately. They did not seem to mind being returned to school early. He realised it was becoming their anchor when their home life was upset. They closed the house up and Peter dropped the boys at school.

Amid their protests, he gave each a hug and jumped in his car with eyes watering. He drove into Bath and called at one of the smaller travel agents. Yes they could get him on a flight to Malaga that evening.

He drove to the hospital, gave Jane a kiss on the cheek and then drove over to the airport. He parked his car in a less obvious space.

He had two hours to wait before take off. Perhaps he should hide in the "Gents". This seemed a little drastic. By the time the Police had organised the operation against the British end of the drugs operation, they would be slow to react to his whereabouts.

That was the chance he would have to take.

Even so he stayed away from the airport building for as long as he could. He walked around the car park and gathered his thoughts. He only went into the 'check in' when he was afraid they would call out his name. If security had been alerted they would check the passenger list for flights to Malaga. Still, there was no point in having his name shouted out.

He walked through to Passport Control and knew this was the test. The duty officer waved him and everyone else through with the usual lack of enthusiasm.

As the plane rolled down the runway he felt elated. He was free. Then the reality dawned on him. He was unlikely to be able to re-enter the country until this business was cleared up.

CHAPTER 27

Supt. Reynolds called his specialist team together. That same evening the electronics specialist slipped into the mews garage with a skeleton key and installed the Electronic Surveillance Device under the floor of the Porsche. The Superintendent went home, secure in the knowledge that the car could be tracked anywhere in the country.

The next morning he arranged for a room to be taken over in the office of a garage across the road. The Surveillance Officers set up their tripods for binoculars and camera, both with infra red lens.

He said 'As soon as someone approaches that garage, get his picture and have it run through the identity computer. After that, your job is over. On no account approach the scene. The ESD boys will take over from there'.

As the two officers settled into the cramped little room for what could possibly be weeks on end, one said 'He's a great motivator, that Supt. Reynolds. As soon as it gets interesting he takes over'.

The Superintendent rang the Inspector in Bristol who was responsible for the function of the ESD monitor. He said

'I want you to set up your gear in Bath station and I want exclusive use until I release you from it'.

'The Inspector said 'That's an impossible request Sir'.

Supt. Reynolds replied 'It's not a request it's an order' and put the phone down, his mind already on the next move.

He spoke to the Control Room and said 'Issue a warrant for the arrest of one Peter Haynes', and gave the address. Get a search warrant and take that house apart'.

Peter walked out of Malaga airport and it was already dark. The warm breeze touched his cheek and he felt good to be back in the warm. He took a taxi into town. The place was humming with activity, horns blaring, neon lights flashing and every bar and restaurant seemed full.

He chose a hotel away from the mainstream and smiled at his predictability. Although he was caught up in more excitement, intrigue and crime than a lot of people in Malaga tonight, he still preferred to keep a low profile.

He was shown to a non-descript but adequate room and asked for a salad and some beer. He knew he must report to Julian as if everything was normal. Gradually he formed his plan.

Meanwhile at his home in England, Police officers were ringing the doorbell. They reported the fact that the house was empty.

Cursing his own slow thinking Supt. Reynolds issued the order to check the airport outgoing passenger lists. 'Search the house anyway' he added.

His department soon provided the information that Peter Haynes had flown to Malaga.

'Inform PC Enfield of this' was the terse reply.

The surveillance team in Pulteney Mews watched people come and go to the garages. Their photographic equipment stood ready but no one entered the garage they were interested in. As darkness fell, one officer gazed relentlessly through infrared binoculars while the other dozed in a chair.

Quietly a car stopped outside the courtyard and a heavily built man got out of the passenger side. He glanced up and down the road then walked quickly to the garage. The Surveillance Officer clicked his camera in rapid succession waking the other officer. As the Porsche crept out of the garage the officer radioed the Vehicle Monitoring Unit in case they were not watching their screens.

The inspector was faced with the decision of whether or not to alert the Superintendent. He made the call and knew he would answer instantly as if he never slept.

The Superintendent listened to the Inspector's report and paused before replying.

'Where is the Porsche now?'

'Heading up the A46, Sir?' My guess is he is going up the M4 to London'.

'Do we have any decipherable photographs of the driver?'

'Yes Sir. Obviously it was dark but if someone knew him, I think they could identify him'.

The Superintendent said 'Call in PC Enfield and ask him if he knows the driver. If we are lucky, it is the villain who took the rap for the road accident that started this whole thing'.

The Porsche turned east towards London as predicted and drove at precisely 70mph as coaches and lorries passed by.

Barny's considerable bulk was uncomfortable at the wheel of the Porsche but he drove as discreetly as possible to avoid attracting attention. In less than two hours the little blip on the monitoring screen approached Chiswick flyover. The Superintendent phoned his opposite number in the Metropolitan Flying Squad.

'You can expect a red Porsche to rendezvous with others shortly for a drugs delivery. See if your ESD unit can pick it up on their screen'

Superintendent Nelson laughed down the phone 'Of course we can track it. My staff will patch in to your computer; simple as that. The operator watched as the Porsche came off the Motorway and into Fulham.

CHAPTER 28

Supt. Nelson issued his orders for three special armoured vans, each containing six officers, to be ready. Each man was armed with a machine pistol and wearing his flak jacket.

The Porsche turned into a side road with a 'Dead End' sign and turned again to face some wire mesh gates. Barney flashed his headlights three times and then switched off all lights.

The gates were opened and he drove into an old disused warehouse. The metal doors opened then closed behind him and the overhead lights came on.

Barney got out of the car, stretched, and walked over to a Portacabin. He opened the door and the hot smoky atmosphere hit him in the face. One man got up from his chair and the other five continued their card game. His dark blue suit and olive coloured skin made him look every inch the gangster he was.

'All OK Barney?'

'Yes Al, no problems'.

'Go to it boys' said Al. The men left the Portacabin and started jacking up the Porsche. Al put a case on the table and opened it to show Barney. The bank notes all used and in rubber bands filled the case. 'It's all there Barney, but count it if you want. Stay for a cup of tea while my men check the merchandise, if you know what I mean'.

Meanwhile a Police Officer looked cautiously through the gates. He could see chinks of light coming from the warehouse.

Stepping clear of the gates he made a windmill motion with his arm in the unmistakable gesture of advance.

The first van charged at the gates, bursting them open, and sped up to the warehouse doors. The other vans took up position and all Police took what cover they could.

The Inspector in charge of the raid shouted through his loud hailer 'Attention you in the warehouse. Come out with your hands held high. The building is surrounded by armed Police Officers'.

Al spoke quietly to his men. 'Keep calm and finish unloading the car. They

145

won't attempt to raid yet. I will break out the artillery'.

Barney watched in amazement as explosives with 3-minute timers were placed around the building.

The Inspector continued his shouted orders, comfortable in the knowledge that they could not escape. But he also knew that to storm the building was to invite casualties.

For a moment it was a stand off and he decided it might be better to wait for daylight.

He shouted again 'We have all night, if necessary. All week, if you like. You've got to come out sometime'.

He returned to his van and radioed his Superintendent. 'We have them cornered in the old warehouse just off the Fulham Road sir. It looks like we sit and wait'.

The Superintendent said 'What about a rear entrance?'

'There isn't one Sir. I know this building. All that is out the back is a pond of stagnant water about forty metres wide. I think it was used for pumping cooling water to machinery years ago. There is no door and these villains won't want to get their expensive suits dirty anyway'.

'OK Inspector, sit it out'.

Inside the warehouse, silent, well-organised activity was under way. The Porsche was being stripped down from bumper to bumper. The packets of drugs were stacked neatly on an old table. The previous night, at the rear of the building, one of Al's men had cut a man-size hole in the corrugated iron wall. A human chain started passing the packets out through to someone in a rubber dingy. When all the drugs were aboard he flashed a pencil torch just once and a rope tightened, coming out of the water. Across the pond, through a hole in a similar building, eager hands pulled the dinghy.

Inside the warehouse a Transit van was parked. The side windows were blacked out and on the side was emblazoned 'Metropolitan Police'. Fitted to the roof was the usual blue light.

The drugs were quietly loaded. Al motioned to his men to leave the building and wait for him in the Police van.

Barney said 'What about me?'

Al replied 'It bothers me that the Police were hot on your tail Barney'.

'What do you mean by that Al?'

Al stepped quietly forward and plunged a stiletto knife into Barney's stomach.

Unexpectedly Barney let out a loud scream as he slipped to his knees.

Al ran for the hole in the wall, jumped into the dinghy and made for the Police van, taking the case full of cash with him. The Inspector hearing the scream, and already uneasy about the long period of quiet, jumped into one of the vans and charged the metal doors.

On impact the whole building exploded! The first Police van was blown backwards into one of the back up vans.

The explosion killed the officer and his driver instantly. What was left of the building collapsed in a pile of dust and smoke over the Porsche and Barney.

The one remaining Police van driver called for back up as he reversed out of the yard. Police vehicles converged on the area with blue lights flashing and sirens wailing.

Als' van mingled with them and then quietly left the area.

CHAPTER 29

Peter woke to the warm sun on his face and for a moment wondered where he was.

The little hotel room became familiar and he showered and dressed then picked up the phone to Julian.

'I'm back and wonder if someone would pick me up'. He gave directions and walked down to the coffee shop.

Julian came himself looking very pre-occupied. 'How did the trip go?' he asked.

'Fine. The Porsche went like a bird and I had a good time with the boys. I put the car in the Mews garage as per instructions'.

Julian even remembered to ask after Jane but his question seemed an afterthought.

He said little during their drive to the villa. He had not received the customary phone call from Barney saying 'Transaction complete'. They drove up to the villa front door and Julian went straight to his office and closed the door. He dare not phone his London contacts as it was agreed this could not happen under any circumstances. He came out of his office and found Peter in the swimming pool. Putting on a brave face, he said 'After lunch I am due at a meeting in Puerto Banus. Would you go over to the architect's office and check progress there?'

With Peter out of the way Julian drove quickly back to town in the new white Mercedes convertible that he had on trial from the garage. He walked quickly to the newsagents and picked up the now one day old Daily Express. There was no need to look further than the front page, LONDON EXPLOSION - TWO POLICE OFFICERS DEAD. DRUG DEALERS SUSPECTED. He bought the paper and sat on a seat to read it.

'Following investigations into drug smuggling activity, Police swooped on a disused warehouse in Fulham. It appears that explosives were placed in the building and the Police drove straight into the trap. Two officers were killed instantly and several more are in hospital.

The area has been sealed off but our staff also spotted from the road the burnt out remains of a car identified by our reporter as a Porsche 911. They also saw Paramedics bring someone out of the rubble on a stretcher.

The Police are not issuing any details regarding this person. They have also said they are mystified as to how the gang escaped as they are confident they sealed off all possible routes'.

Julian went back to his car and drove to the public telephone facility in Puerto Banus harbour. He phoned the London number that he had committed to memory but never written down. A cultured voice said cautiously 'Hello'.

'I hear there have been complications with our recent delivery'.

'I told you never to call me here'.

'At the moment I have neither goods or payment and possibly one of my senior staff out of circulation'.

The cultured voice replied 'You must appreciate that we, as customers, expect our suppliers to run a smooth operation and would recommend that your representative here in London is contacted by our own staff to clear up the difficulty'.

He went on to say 'Following that I would suggest that you arrange a further shipment and provided that is carried out satisfactorily we will organise payment for both shipments to be made together'.

Julian said 'My Company could not finance such an arrangement'.

'Then we cannot transact further business and any outstanding monies will be forfeited by yourselves. We are a highly respected organisation in the City of London and I cannot think you will entertain complaining to the authorities'.

A manicured hand replaced the telephone receiver. He leant back in his leather chair and gazed out of the window at the Thames for a moment. Then he pressed the button on his internal phone. 'Miss Gibbs, ask the Head of Security to report to me please'. Puzzled that the Chairman should wish to speak to security staff, the girl paused but answered 'Yes Sir'.

The Head of Security knocked on the Chairman's door and entered upon a one word command - 'Come'.

He stood in front of the large mahogany desk, uncomfortable in the opulent office.

The distinguished gentleman looked at the man before him and said 'It would appear all did not go as planned'.

His conversation never gave any clues as to the actual business being done as if he feared he could be overheard. 'Although I see no reason to panic, I think we should clear up the odd loose ends. Would you please arrange for a member of staff to visit the sick'.

'Yes Sir' replied Head of Security. He returned to his own office on a lower floor and called in Alan Sopiro. 'Al, we need to finish what you started. Find out where Barney is.

CHAPTER 30

Several phone calls later and promises of favours and reminders of favours given, Al had his information. He also found out that Barney was in a critical condition and that his room at the hospital had a guard outside.

He used one of his chirpy sounding girls to ring the hospital. She said 'You have a badly burned man in hospital and we want to send some flowers. What room is he in please?' The Receptionist looked down the admissions and saw the red star against the name. 'We cannot issue that information but bring them to reception and I will see he gets them'.

The Head of Security gave the girl her instructions. She drove to the hospital and handed the flowers to the receptionist. She hung around in the reception area and soon enough an orderly came for them.

She discreetly followed him through the corridor, up one flight of steps and into a ward of private rooms. Outside of one room sat a security guard. The girl walked past the room and glanced at the number on the door - 103. She walked on past two more, 104 and 105.

She turned round and walked back to the top of the stairs and looked out the window onto the car park. She lined up her sight with two shrubs exactly one behind the other. Returning to the car park she went to the shrub furthest from the window. She lined it up with the wall of windows. Her line of sight lined up with one window. She had identified the window of room 103.

That same afternoon a new window cleaner began to clean the first floor windows and on reaching number 103, slipped the catch on the sash window with a flat blade knife. He crept into the room and slid two wedges under the door, inches from the security guard outside. He could do nothing about the window in the door, but hope.

The guard would be looking to stop people going in, not anyone coming out of the room. At the bedside he produced a hypodermic needle and injected the motionless Barney in the arm.

The drug would cause death in about 15 minutes giving Al Soporo time to slip away before the automatic monitoring equipment gave the alarm. He calmly put the protective cap on to the needle and put the hypodermic in the top pocket of his window cleaner's overalls. Continuing on all fours he slipped the wedges out from under the door and put them in his pocket. With luck the doctors would attribute the death to the wound and burns sustained previously.

The urbane Bank Chairman took the phone call from Head of Security who simply said 'The patient is terminally ill and will not last the night'.

CHAPTER 31

Peter was quick to realise that Julian wanted him out of the way that day and took the opportunity to visit Manuel at the farm. He told Manuel the story to date and said

'Something is wrong, I can feel it'.

Manuel said 'This man Julian must be wondering about you. Business was going well until he sent you to London. I thought of you Peter when I read the newspaper this morning. You see, I read the English paper if I go into Marbella. A bar I use is run by an Englishman and he keeps his newspaper for me'. He recounted what he could remember and most importantly the burnt out Porsche.

'What will you do now' he asked Peter.

'All I can do is wait for Julian's next move' Peter replied. 'I must get back to the villa'.

As he was leaving Manuel said 'I have purchased a new 'toy' and he showed him his mobile telephone. He wrote down the number for Peter. Unexpectedly Manuel stood up and put his arm around Peter's shoulders saying 'Go on back to the villa, act normally, phone home and check on your wife and sons. That will make you feel better'.

Peter drove thoughtfully back to find Julian with Danny and Tony. He handed the newspaper to Peter and watched him read it. 'What do you know about this?' he demanded.

Peter feigning shock and indignation raised his voice 'You didn't tell me I was driving a car full of drugs home'.

Julian stared at Peter and spoke slowly. 'I am well out of pocket on this deal and my customers do not want to do business any more unless I prove I have sorted things out.

Somehow we must get another shipment organised'.

Peter said 'I do not want to get further involved with this'.

Julian replied 'You can't go home; the Police may well be looking for you. Anyway you are one of the team and we stick together'.

Peter said 'I'm out and you can't make me stay'.

Julian nodded and Tony leapt forward and drove his fingers straight into Peter's solar plexus. As he doubled over Tony slapped him several times around the head. He shoved him into a chair.

'Do as you are told, no one deserts me. Don't forget one phone call from me and your two sons will not reach manhood. I have tried to be good to you and as soon as the going gets rough you want out'.

Peter, recovering quickly in the chair, leapt to his feet and lunged at Julian. Tony was quicker and hit Peter accurately with a karate chop to the neck and Peter was out cold.

Julian said 'Lock him in here and he can reflect on his position. If he knows something we will get it out of him later. I must now arrange to purchase more merchandise and our suppliers may have to wait for payment, this time'.

A few minutes later Peter came round rubbing his neck. He sat on the floor, still livid at the threat to his boys.

After about half an hour the lock turned in the door and Julian walked in alone. 'I am sorry about all that. We are all on edge and the best way forward is to get this shipment done and then we will be paid'. Peter said 'You threatened my boys'.

'Heat of the moment old boy'.

Tony walked in and offered his hand 'No hard feelings I hope'.

'No, none' lied Peter. Tony relaxed shaking Peter's hand. As he came in range Peter brought his knee up swiftly between Tony's legs and as he bent over in agony, Peter returned the karate chop he had suffered. Tony fell motionless.

Peter looked up and studied the Walther PPK pistol in Julian's hand. Peter said 'That's the end of the matter as far as I am concerned. But I won't be pushed around by anyone'.

'I will remember that' said Julian putting the gun away.

Julian arranged for the four of them to have dinner at the villa while he informed them of the plan. Tony eyed Peter warily as the Spanish girl brought cold meat, olives, cheeses and wine. Julian felt the tensions round the table and said 'I will not have any more squabbling. We have a lot at stake, concentrate on that'. Danny always the quiet mysterious one saw Peter looking at him and lifted an eyebrow slightly. I wonder if I have an ally there, thought Peter.

Peter now knew that Julian had a gun and maybe Danny and Tony did too. He had been roughed up expertly by Tony and would not get caught unawares again.

The newspaper article told him that people had been killed in London. The source of drugs was Tangier and the purchasers were in London. Originally his only thought was to expose Julian. He must co-operate with Julian until the chance for his revenge presented itself. So far the only man he could rely on was Manuel.

The next day they were told to report to the yacht by 3pm. Peter drove into Puerto Banus in the morning and went into the public car park, checking that the big Nissan was parked up the side street as he did so. He drove on into Marbella town and purchased a mobile phone. He knew he could explain this by saying he wanted to be in constant touch with his family. He bought the Express newspaper looking for any further news.

'Fulham Explosion Claims Another Life - A man believed to be one of the drug dealers has died in hospital'. Peter wondered who it was.

The day before, a very thorough Doctor at the hospital studied the medical record thoughtfully. 'A stab wound in the stomach and extensive burns. Serious yes, but life threatening? Possibly not'. He ordered a post mortem.

Peter folded up the newspaper and was surprised to see Danny walking towards him.

'Is this a coincidence Danny?'

'Between ourselves' Danny replied 'I was told to follow you. I may as well tell you Julian doesn't trust you. Tony is putting further doubts in his mind and you have made yourself an enemy there'.

'What about you Danny?'

'I have made a lot of money working for Julian but it's getting a bit too hot for me now. But like you I'm in deep'.

'What can you tell me Danny?'

'Just look out for yourself, that's all'.

Danny walked away. Tony watched all this from a safe distance and would report that Danny had talked to Peter.

Later they all met on board as planned and busied themselves preparing for sea. Julian had dared not ask his suppliers for time to pay. They would laugh in his face, but as always he had a plan.

As darkness descended 'Paradise' crept quietly out of the harbour and began its long cruise down the coast. Julian, withdrawn and tense, sat at the controls saying nothing. Peter wandered out on deck feeling the cool breeze through his silk shirt. Leaning on the guardrail he watched the slight swell of the waves and thought of the mystery in those dark depths.

Danny called out to him. 'There is a cup of coffee for you on the bridge'. He joined the other three and Julian said 'This is what we do. We don't have the money to pay for this shipment. When the drugs are aboard we are going to blow up the other boat and shoot any survivors - any questions?'

Peter felt his jaw drop and the colour drained from his cheeks. He clutched the seat beside him. Julian pointed to a box of grenades and four machine pistols. 'As soon as the paravane is winched clear of the launch, I will go to full power and hard to port so be ready or you will fall overboard. You three will have grenades in your hand and your guns slung around your backs. Don't worry, they won't see you in the gloom'. There was no way out for Peter and he tried to console himself by saying repeatedly to himself 'They are only drug runners'. He had been in combat before, of course, when on active service. But this was going to be slaughter.

The launch came quietly up to them without lights as before. The drugs were passed quickly on board and stacked into the paravane. Tony closed the cover on the paravane and flicked his torch on and off to Julian on the bridge. He spun the wheel hard to port and then the throttles to full power.

Tony opened fire with the machine pistol, spitting yellow flame as he raked the launch and crew with a hail of bullets. He let go of the gun and threw his grenade into the launch. Danny did the same and yelled to Peter to throw his. In that split second Peter knew that the crew could not survive anyway so he threw the grenade in an over arm lob into the launch.

Paradise leapt forward digging the stern into the sea in a welter of foam. Only a few yards separated the boats when the launch evaporated in a mushroom of yellow flame. The close range explosion blew Peter and his fellow murderers back against the superstructure of Paradise. The night air was filled with debris and smoke and as they sped away into the night bits were falling on to their deck. Half stunned and sick with what he had done, Peter was showered with flecks of clothing and splatterings of flesh and blood. He clung to the rail for a moment and swallowed hard. The yacht slowed as Julian began to turn her round. He shouted 'It's raining men'. 'Let's have a look'. They went back into the area and there were bits of wood still smoking, drifting gently on the waves. Peter called 'There, look, one of the crew'. What remained of the engine cover panel was partially submerged by a body charred and blackened with clothes burnt into the flesh. As a wave lifted the panel an arm moved as if beckoning to them. Tony fired a long burst and Peter could hear the bullets thudding into the body. It slid quietly beneath the waves.

Danny said 'Don't feel too bad, I am sure he was already dead'.

Peter quickly headed for the bridge on impulse. Julian seemed ready for him, his gun on his lap just in case.

He spoke first 'Don't say a word, I don't need a lecture'. Peter studied his face, shining with sweat. He was flushed with excitement, eyes flashing, that hard mouth almost smiling'. 'You look like you enjoyed that'.

'I was looking forward to it' Julian replied. He dialled a number on the bridge telephone.

'There's been an accident. We accepted our delivery and paid over the money as usual. A few minutes later there was an almighty bang and your men's launch blew up. We have returned to the scene but no one could have survived that. Yes the money was on board. Is there anything we can do? OK, I am very sorry. We will leave the area now, as the authorities no doubt saw the flames'.

Julian turned on the power and headed out to sea. On deck Danny was hosing the yacht down while Tony was preparing to lower the paravane into the water.

Peter joined them and busied himself with them. He took off his shirt and threw it overboard and Danny hosed him down as well. He went below and put on clean clothes. Feeling the Paradise cruise in a wide arc he went up on deck and saw the paravane being lowered over the side to take up its position beneath the keel of the yacht. Julian turned on the navigation lights. Guns were hidden away and Danny produced brandies all round. By the time they reached Puerto Banus in the early hours, life aboard looked normal. Julian turned the yacht and lined up stern first as always. No one wanted to stay aboard the yacht so Julian decided everyone should return to the villa.

CHAPTER 32

Alone at last in his room Peter wanted to talk to his only ally in this mess. He went into the en-suite bathroom and turned on the shower. Dialling Manuel's number he hoped the noise of running water would mask his voice. He recounted the events to date and Manuel took it all in although it was very early in the morning and not yet light.

He said 'Peter, it's time to call the Police, this is more than you can handle'.

The door of the bathroom opened quietly and Julian reached in and turned off the shower. Peter felt the sudden silence and spun round.

Julian held the gun steady and pointing at Peter's stomach said 'Who are you calling'. 'Manuel' Peter said truthfully.

'That's the last call you'll make' and that sinister smile came over his face.

'Tony' he shouted 'Take this gutless wonder out in the hills and get rid of him'.

Tony prodded Peter in the ribs and they all went out into the courtyard. With Julian's gun still trained on him Peter was pushed into the Jeep and handcuffed to the roll bar so he could barely sit down. Tony put his machine pistol on his lap and drove off with Peter's hands handcuffed above his head.

Tony said 'You're headed for a nice hot deep ravine, my friend, and I hope you take a long time to die'.

Peter's arms began to ache and his wrists were chaffing as the Jeep bounced along. He tried to take some of the strain off his arms by driving his legs up under him but Tony put one hand on the gun and shouted 'keep still'. For a few minutes Peter did keep still then leapt up like a coiled spring and kicked Tony hard in the side of the head. The Jeep swerved and went up on two wheels. Tony literally flew out onto the rock strewn hard ground. The Jeep went all the way over and back on its wheels.

As it rolled, the back of Peter's hands and fingers grazed heavily on the ground. He hung from the roll bar dazed. Tony was on his hands and knees. The leather strap from the gun had caught around the gear stick in the roll. Peter nudged the gun up between his knees and hung his head down as far as he could. By turning the gun he got his teeth onto the strap. The weight of it made his jaw crack and sweat and blood from his grazed face ran into his eyes.

Tony's head was beginning to clear and he turned slowly and began to drag himself on all fours towards the jeep. Peter squirmed and wriggled until his hands were on the gun. He aimed as best he could manacled to the bar and fired. The earth in front of Tony erupted, and he stopped crawling. Tony said 'You haven't got the guts to shoot me'.

'All I'll do is shoot you in the legs. You won't die but it will keep you out of mischief'.

'What do you want me to do?'

'Stay on your hands and knees and come over here. Put the keys to these handcuffs where I can reach them. That's it, now back off'. Peter balanced the gun on the top of the windshield and picked up the key. For the first time he noticed the state of his hands and wrists but still felt no pain. He turned the key, released the handcuffs, and lowered his arms. He knew now that the pain would come as the circulation returned. Picking up the gun he looked at Tony who sat looking back at him. 'I don't like you any more than you like me but I am in this too deep to go to the Police. You are going to drive me back to the main road and then we split up. I don't care whether you tell Julian I am dead or alive. I am getting out of Spain as fast as I can'.

Tony drove while Peter sat in the passenger seat pointing the gun at him. 'Pull in here Tony'. He handcuffed Tony to the roll bar just as he had been. Then he put the key on the back seat in full view. 'See if you can attract the attention of anyone going by. I'm off'.

What Tony did not know was that it was a track off this main road that led to Manuel's farm.

Peter strode back down the road feeling the cuts and bruises all over. He knew if a car came by he could just jump into the bushes. He did not want a lift or he would need to explain the gun. After twenty minutes he found the track he was looking for. He marched on past the spot where he had first met Manuel and remembered for a moment the dry humour of the big Spaniard.

The sun was getting hotter and he did not have any water. His canvas deck shoes were falling apart and his feet were cut. Each time he lost his footing he seemed to stumble into a gorse bush, scratching his arms and tearing his clothes. He practically staggered into the farmyard and sure enough there was Manuel tending the tractor.

Manuel jumped down off the tractor and caught Peter as the last energy drained from him 'It's been one of those nights Manuel'.

As Manuel's wife patched him up he told them of the events on the road. 'You were foolish to leave Tony like that, they will hunt you down and finish the job'.

'They think I am leaving Spain'.

'That is my recommendation to you' replied Manuel.

'If I had killed Tony that would make me as bad as him. Anyway I will need to get to Puerto Banus. How is the tractor?'

'No need for the tractor. I have a little car. I will bring it around to the door'.

Peter walked out to see an old Morris Minor.

'Ees good eh?' asked Manuel.

'For a twenty five year old car, yes I suppose so. But how do you fit in to drive it?'

Manuel opened the driver's door to reveal that the driver's seat was missing. He climbed in and sat on the back seat and assumed a driving position. Peter burst out laughing as he got in the other door. They bounced down the track on to the road and soon saw the lights of the harbour. He directed Manuel to the street where the big Nissan Patrol was parked. There it was looking very forlorn under a thick layer of dust. 'Only problem is I don't have the key'.

Manuel ran his hand along the inner edge of the front bumper and found a little box with the spare key. 'Rental companies always do that for tourists who lose their keys' he chuckled.

If Peter thought correctly Julian would want to get to the yacht to move the drugs as soon as possible and he wanted to be there first. They left the old car and jumped in to the Nissan.

Tony looked at the keys on the back seat of the Jeep. He slid the handcuffs down around the roll bar. Stretching as far as he could he clamped his teeth on to the leather key fob on the rear seat. He brought his mouth up to his hands and his fingers grabbed the keys.

Back at the villa Tony reported that Peter had got the better of him and was leaving Spain as fast as he could. Julian said 'It's possible, but I am not convinced. There is more to that guy than I thought. You've seen him fight and handle a gun. I wonder why he came to Spain. Let's get the cargo shifted before anything else goes wrong'.

They jumped into the Mercedes sports, Danny in the back seat and Tony in the front with Julian. Danny sensed he was out of favour.

Peter drew up on the quay wall, which was a couple of metres higher up than Paradise. He did not have time to immobilise the yacht and guessed Julian would be on his way. The mooring lines were on the port side fore and aft. He jumped out of the Nissan and dragged the steel cable of the winch on the front bumper with him down onto the pontoon.

He looped it around the starboard mooring stanchion and Manuel, quick on the uptake, took up the slack on the winch control.

'That boat is not going anywhere. Manuel you go and get your friends in the Police and I'll stay here. We need to catch them in possession of the drugs'.

Peter jumped back in the Nissan and prayed Julian would not spot the winch cable.

Within minutes the Mercedes came swiftly into view but they had to park a few bays down from the boat. Peter ducked down as low as he could, just peeping over the dashboard. The crew rapidly began preparing for sea and Julian was warming up the engines. Tony stood by the stern mooring rope and Danny the forward one Julian waved his arm and they cast off. Paradise moved forward with the twin diesels purring. The steel winch cable tightened and the stern dug into the water. Julian, not realising anything was wrong, opened the throttles wider and the harbour water was churned to foam. Incredibly the Nissan began to be dragged to the edge of the harbour wall, the back tyres leaving black skid marks as the hand brake held the wheels. Peter had not reckoned on the effect of Paradise being lower than the Nissan and the weight was taken off the back wheels as it was pulled down.

Tony ran to the mooring stanchion, saw the cable, and dashed to the bridge.

'We are held by a steel cable attached to that truck behind us'.

'Don't worry, we'll show them what Paradise can do. Get an axe, we'll pull the truck off the wall and then you cut the cable. They did not notice whose truck it was.

Peter, feeling the Nissan begin to slide, started his engine and slammed into reverse. Julian knowing that a steady pull would leave his propellers spinning in pockets of air, began opening and closing the throttles. Paradise leapt forward and back, lunging like an eager tiger on a leash. The Nissan stood its ground as Peter revved harder and harder. The front of the Nissan pulled down hard on the suspension. Peter saw the winch cable quivering under the strain. He could not believe that the yacht was holding its own. In the engine room the two mighty diesels roared to a deafening pitch. Both men knew something must give.

Julian went to full power and Paradise almost leapt out of the water as the mooring post was ripped from the deck. In a split second Peter ducked down below the dashboard as the steel cable snaked through the air like a bullwhip. The heavy mooring post smashed through the windscreen and showered Peter with glass. Julian powered the yacht out of the moorings towards the harbour exit. He bounced off small craft, the huge bow waves wreaking havoc as he went.

Peter sat up and quickly kicked the rest of the windscreen out, started up and spun the Nissan around. With his hand on the horn he scattered the tourists and made for the highway to Marbella.

As soon as he hit the tarmac he got to the middle of the road, put his headlights and 4 way flashers on, and slammed his foot to the floor. The traffic gave way to the Nissan, detecting he did not intend to stop for anyone. Scarcely taking his eyes off the road he dialled Manuel, hoping against hope that the big Spaniard had his phone with him.

He answered instantly 'Manuel, he's getting away. Can you organise a Police Patrol boat? 'If they have an inshore inflatable tell them to launch immediately and head for the harbour entrance at

Puerto Banus. Tell the Police to wait for me at the Police moorings. They will need all the guns they can get'. Peter switched the phone off before Manuel could reply.

CHAPTER 33

Manuel was already at the Police Port Office and his friend Luis, known to everybody as Skipper, had the necessary authority to organise the chase. The duty officer pressed the siren, which signalled lifeboat crew to man the large rigid inflatable. Within 3 minutes the craft was ready to go, twin Mercury outboard motors already running. He selected two able young Policemen with machine pistols who jumped in the inflatable.

They roared off to sea and swung to starboard running parallel to the coast. With a top speed of over 40 knots the skipper knew they would either meet Paradise quickly or catch up with her if she was sailing away from them. He glanced at the radar but there were so many boats in the area the screen told him nothing.

The green swell lifted the inflatable and they were airborne for long seconds at a time slapping down into the gully between the waves. The two Policemen were holding their safety lines wrapped around one hand with machine pistol in the other. One crew member was in the bows of the craft, sweeping the sea with binoculars.

Within minutes he spotted Paradise outrunning all the other boats and pushing a huge white bow wave before it. As soon as she was in earshot the skipper yelled 'Heave to, Heave to Espana Policia' on his loud hailer.

The yacht kept coming, rapidly closing the gap between them. The inflatable swerved neatly to one side and the bow wave from the yacht nearly swamped them. They turned and ran alongside the Paradise and pulled ahead. A Policeman fired warning shots across the bow. Julian watched from the bridge and shouted to Tony.

'Blow that rubber ring out of the water'.

Tony, down in the Stateroom, ran across the plush carpet and pressed a button on a wall. An impressionist painting slid upwards revealing a panel about a foot wide but only four inches deep. He slid the panel side ways and looked out. The inflatable was bouncing along not 10 yards away. He set his machine gun to automatic fire and pushed the barrel out of the slot. He raked the rubber craft and crew with non-stop gunfire. The four men were killed or mortally wounded.

One Policeman returned fire although he was hit himself. His bullets were making clanging noises against the hull of Paradise. He was the first to learn that the yacht had a steel hull, but the secret was safe. Tony's bullets slapped into him and he was lifted clear out of the craft with the force of them.

He continued to let the bullets pour from his gun, hitting the outboard engines and stopping them. He ran up from the stateroom to the stern deck and threw a grenade towards the inflatable as it fell rapidly behind. The sea erupted and the craft flew into the air in a plume of flame. Tony laughed aloud and joined Julian on the bridge.

It had taken a few more minutes to get the Police Patrol Boat (PPB) under way. Peter clung to the grab handle in the cockpit of the PPB. As they gathered speed the sleek black hull lifted out of the water into the plane position. The surge of power pushed Peter in the back. 'How fast does this boat go?' He asked incredulously. The skipper either did not speak English or was concentrating hard.

Manuel said 'It's never been beaten yet'. As they spoke the ball of flame appeared in the sky. 'Look's like they have met up. Make for the flash' shouted Peter.

The PPB crashed through the waves and the trained crew on deck snapped on lifelines. White spray hit the wheelhouse and the skipper held steady on the point where the inflatable had been hit. 'Reduce speed, there are bodies in the water!' Peter knew instantly whose handiwork this was. The skipper looked ashen and was trembling. Work mates, friends of his, lying in the water like rubbish. Some with limbs torn off still colouring the water with dark arterial blood.

They slowed almost to a stop. Large pieces of rubber from the inflatable were floating all round them. Sudden quiet came over this watery graveyard. Peter cocked an ear to the wind. The heavy drone of the Paradise diesels! He sensed that their bows were pointing in the direction of the engine noise. Glancing at the radar he selected the most likely blip on the screen 'There, go for it' he yelled. The skipper just sat in his cockpit seat, his skin gone from sun tanned to a sickly green.

Peter pulled him roughly from the seat and practically lifted him into Manuel's arms 'Look after him Manuel, he'll come round'. Manuel sat him down in the corner of the wheelhouse.

Peter sat in the skipper's chair and snapped on the safety harness. 'Tell the deck crew we are going flat out to catch the people who did this to their friends. Find out what weapons we have'. His natural ability to take command in a crisis overtook the dazed men around him.

Peter thrust the throttle to full speed and even in these dangerous and tragic circumstances he was thrilled by the power. He knew that he could catch them. Manuel reappeared in the doorway. 'We have a deck mounted machine gun, machine pistols, flares, and wait for it, what looks like a rocket launcher'.

'Right, tell the crew what to expect - you are the interpreter'. The PPB pounded its way through the waves. Where the skipper was riding with the sea, Peter refused to yield, and put his trust in the strength of the boat. Manuel had the presence of mind to shout to the crew to get off the deck. They did not need telling twice. They had not ridden with anyone who ran the PPB at this speed. The sea was getting darker and little white flecks of foam were flying off the tops of the waves. The PPB lifted clear of the water and crashed down into the next trough with a deafening crash.

'Enough to split us in two' thought Peter. As they approached the next big wave the PPB only lifted a little, the sheer speed pushing her through the wall of water. A dark green silent world surrounded them for an instant but she was quickly through it and the automatic bilge pumps began to work.

The skipper was recovering and pulled himself to his feet and shouted 'My boat, she will break up, slow down, slow down'. Peter shrugged him off and held his hand firmly on the throttles 'So you can speak English!'

In between the waves hitting them the Paradise came into view. Considering she was also at maximum speed the PPB was doing well. Peter knew he had to get in front to stand any chance of stopping her. He gradually overtook Paradise and could see Julian in the cockpit. Snatching the microphone he yelled 'Paradise, heave to, heave to, we can outrun you and are heavily armed'. Surprisingly Paradise began to slow and Peter did the same, staying out of range of small arms fire.

The boats began to roll in the swell as Peter released his safety harness and handed the PPB back to its rightful skipper. Julian's voice carried across the waves 'Come any closer and we will open fire. Tell your crew to stay below or we open fire. We know we are caught and will turn around and make for Marbella harbour. Keep your distance'.

Paradise came about and at a much reduced speed headed for home. Peter tried to watch the activity on the bridge but it was too far away. Julian called Danny up and said 'Take the helm Danny. It looks like the game is up'. Danny, thankful the killing was over sat in the leather seat. Julian walked behind him to go below. As he did so, he slugged Danny on the side of the head with his gun. Danny slumped unconscious and Julian snapped on the harness to keep him in the seat. He switched to automatic pilot and set the pilot for Marbella harbour. Jumping down the steps he joined Tony in the diving compartment hold and they both stripped and put on wet suits and diving gear.

Julian gave the thumbs up and Tony pressed the red button beside him. The hold filled with water very quickly with the speed of the boat and they began to breathe through their oxygen tanks.

The rush of water was deafening and they were blind in the foam of bubbles but they knew the paravane was beneath them. Julian held a remote controller secured with a loop round his wrist. Bracing themselves with hands and feet around the side walls of the hold he pressed the controller. The paravane plunged down into the sea and they let themselves go through the same hatch. They had less than five seconds to dive below the propellers as the boat carried on. The huge steel bands guarding the propellers brushed them aside and they settled in the water. After a couple of minutes they swam down until they saw the paravane on the seabed. Julian worked the controller and the big metal fish began to come towards them. They aimed the priceless cargo to the surface of the sea and joined it there. Bobbing in the waves Julian lifted his mask and saw the two boats already a long way off. 'Tony we have a long swim home but the paravane will pull us along. We will head straight for the nearest piece of coast and hide the drugs while we decide what to do'.

CHAPTER 34

Peter said to Manuel 'This is too easy for my liking'. He picked up the microphone 'Paradise, increase your speed, it will take all night like this'. No reply. 'Paradise, I repeat, increase speed to 15 knots'. 'Something is wrong'. 'Skipper, we need a volunteer to fire a warning shot'. The skipper spoke into his intercom and two men ran along the deck and pulled the cover off the deck mounted machine gun. They fired three rounds in rapid succession. No response. 'Skipper, move in closer'. They ran cautiously alongside. Now all guns on the PPB were trained on the Paradise. Peter could see the figure hunched in the wheelhouse. 'We need to board her somehow'. The skipper put his hand on Peter's shoulder.

'My crew will do it, it is dangerous and they are used to it'. They came as close as they dared and lowered fenders along the Police launch. A muscular crewman in T-shirt and jeans threw a grappling iron onto the bow of Paradise and it slid and clanged along the deck and then hooked onto the guardrail. Expertly, the skipper inched closer to the yacht and the two boats bobbed up and down almost in unison.

As the gap drew narrower the crewman leapt nimbly across and immediately released the grappling hook. He ran for the wheelhouse and found Danny still unconscious. Grabbing the throttle he shut down the engines and hit the red override button on the autopilot. Paradise began to wallow in the swell. The crewman turned to Danny and saw the wound on the side of his head and checked his pulse. He returned to the deck and yelled in Spanish to his skipper 'One man unconscious. No one else aboard unless hiding. Autopilot was operating'. This was a trained man giving vital information rapidly.

Manuel translated the message to Peter who requested he board Paradise. The skipper closed the gap and he and Manuel jumped across and searched the yacht but Danny was the only man aboard. The crewman took the helm and they sloshed cold water into Danny's face. He began to come round and Peter demanded 'Where's Julian?'

'All I know is he was here with Tony and someone must have hit me from behind' Danny replied.

Realising and respecting that Danny would still have some loyalty to his old boss, however misguided; he did not press him further. 'Manuel, he was here, he could not swim to shore in a pair of shorts. It's too far and too cold'. They went below and looked around. The Stateroom with its opulent décor reminded Peter of that first dinner with Julian. They returned to Danny. 'You know you are going to jail Danny. Do you want to help and we will try to make things easier for you?' Danny just nodded and rubbed his no doubt aching head. 'There is an underwater hatch to gain access to the paravane. With wet suits and breathing apparatus they could have got away and hitched a lift on the paravane. Julian has a remote controller to guide it'.

'Thanks Danny'. Peter put a hand on his shoulder. With Danny's help they tried to track the paravane and override the remote control but it was out of range.

CHAPTER 35

Julian and Tony clung doggedly to the fins of the paravane, feeling cold even through the wet suits. The metal cut into their hands. Julian knew that by keeping his wrist compass pointing west the lights of Marbella harbour would appear to their left and they would be able to beach nearby. As the sea became shallower, they stopped and wedged the paravane into the rocks. They piled more rocks over it.

Surfacing quietly they swam to the little beach and made a mental note of the hiding place. Taking off their diving gear they rubbed their limbs to warm up. 'All we need to do now is ring our customers who will arrange collection'.

Tony said 'Look Julian, the Police are hunting us and Paradise is in their hands by now or sunk unmanned.' 'I have been thinking about that while enjoying my long swim' Julian replied. 'Put your trust in me. We are going to the Police station'.

They walked along the beach and up the steps to the coast road. Dressed only in shorts they hitched a lift to the Harbour Police Station. By the wharf they spotted Paradise tied up and walked towards it. Danny was being escorted away in handcuffs. Peter and Manuel stood open mouthed as Julian and Tony came aboard. Quickly Peter told the Police who was coming. Julian said 'I am glad to see you. I know you were chasing Paradise. We were held at gunpoint all the way and they made me lead you on over the loud hailer'.

'Who's they?'

'Drug runners commandeered our boat'.

'How did you get away?

'Just dived over the side' replied Julian.

'You are very good swimmers then' said Manuel.

A police officer stepped forward 'You are under arrest' and handcuffed Julian and Tony.

'We were held at gun point and only just got away with our lives and you arrest us?'

They were led away to a prison cell within the Police station where they joined Danny. The skipper said to Peter and Manuel 'You can go now, leave a telephone number for us to contact you'.

Manuel said 'Come up to the farm' and climbed into his Morris Minor. Peter walked over to the Nissan and wondered what he would say to the hire company as he surveyed the damage.

Driving out from the harbour he noticed wryly that the air conditioning was not needed without the windscreen in place.

The climb out of Marbella into the hills was slow work for the Morris Minor and Peter had ample time to reflect on his action filled day. Why did Julian give himself up? Is it possible he thinks he can get away with killing people? Surely the murder of Police officers in Spain is looked upon as seriously as it is in the UK. Maybe they will just let them rot in one of those notorious Spanish gaols. Peter's thoughts continued until they drove into the farmyard.

Julian sat with Tony and Danny in his cold cell with just a blanket round his shoulders. He guessed that they would be moved to a major Police station quickly as the Harbour Police reported their arrest. Tony spoke 'I suppose you have a plan to get us out of this?'

'I am going to try Tony. Just be ready, they will move us soon'. They looked at one another for a few moments. Julian called to the guard sat outside the cell.

'I am entitled to one phone call'.

'No English' the guard replied.

'Then fetch someone who speaks English'. He spelt out his request in monosyllables several times. Eventually the guard called someone. 'I am entitled to one phone call' Julian repeated. 'You are entitled to nothing, murderer'. Replied the officer.

'We have done nothing wrong and when we are released you will be in trouble.

What is your name?'

'My name is for my friends' the English-speaking officer replied.

'OK, then phone the number I give you, which is my solicitor, tell him where you are sending us'.

The policeman said 'Give me the telephone number' and Julian repeated it from memory.

Julian winked at Tony 'Let's get some rest, that was a long swim'.

The policeman, out of curiosity rather than anything else, dialled the number. A male voice answered too quickly for the policeman to catch the name of the firm. 'I am calling on behalf of Julian Wilding. Do you know him?'

'Yes, I act for him'.

'He is held here at Marbella Harbour Police Station on very serious charges, Murder of Police Officers'.

'Have you charged him officially?'

'No'.

'Then do not do so until I arrive'. The solicitor replaced the receiver and consulted his little book of telephone numbers. He dialled quickly and a very senior officer of Marbella Central Police answered his priv -ate phone. 'I am calling on behalf of Julian Wilding whom I believe is well known to you'.

'Yes'.

'He is held at the Harbour Police Station on allegations of a very serious crime that he did not commit'.

'Who are you'?

'His solicitor'

'What is the allegation?'

'Murder of several Police Officers'.

'I cannot help him then'.

'Julian has been extremely good to you, do I have to spell it out?'

'Yes you do' the senior police officer replied.

The solicitor played his trump card 'I am looking at a photograph of you at a party on board a yacht called Paradise. It is one thing to pose for a picture with a pretty girl on deck but I am more interested in this picture, which looks to be taken in a cabin of the boat. That girl looks to be about nine years old. I have other pictures here, leaving nothing to the imagination'.

The police officer mopped his brow with his handkerchief. The solicitor could hear the coarse, gasping breath on the other end of the phone and pressed home the advantage. 'Meet me at the Harbour Police Station and I will give you the photograph collection when we come out with Julian and his assistants. Let's say two hours from now, shall we?'

'OK' He replied.

CHAPTER 36

Julian lay with his hands behind his head and listened to the snatches of English and Spanish.

'What are the charges? Who witnessed all this? You say Danny was aboard the yacht, alone, which is he? You allowed a hill farmer and an unknown Englishman to commandeer our patrol boats? These two men walked into this Police Station, having got away and you arrest them? It is you who should be locked up'.

The senior officer thumped the desk, waved his arms and shouted, waving his finger in front of the Harbour Police Officer.

'Release these men, they are known to me personally. Their yacht is registered in Puerto Banus and if they can help with this matter I know they will'. Turning to the solicitor 'I will require their passports until further notice'. Julian, Tony and Danny walked free into the street. Tony said 'Why confiscate the passports, they are not even required these days'.

'That's why we didn't object' said the solicitor.

'What was in the envelope you gave him?

'Oh, just holiday photographs he wanted. Don't worry the negatives are in my safe still. I hope you didn't mind, I put an IOU note in there as well'. 'I trust you will honour it'. 'As always' replied Julian.

The skipper who was in charge of the PPB stood dumbfounded as his captives left the building. Returning to his office he dialled the number Manuel had given him. 'Yes, that's right, released without charge. I expect they will collect the yacht and return to Puerto Banus'.

Peter said 'This must mean Julian has senior police officers on his payroll. Let's think back, they off loaded the drugs somewhere before Paradise was boarded. Do you think they will go back for them?'

'Not straight away' replied Manuel.

Manuel took the initiative and picked up his phone. 'Skipper, could you arrange for someone to keep an eye on the yacht Paradise? We expect it to sail back to

Puerto Banus. Can you observe it from there?' Skipper agreed.

Julian and his two assistants brought Paradise out of Marbella Harbour and turned to starboard towards Puerto Banus.

Julian said to Danny, 'I'm sorry I slugged you but you knew I would get you out, didn't you?'

'No I didn't' Danny said quietly.

'Well as you well know I demand 100% loyalty Danny and I give the same back. Stay with me and you share the spoils. Try to leave me and you will die. Is that clear enough for you?'

'Yes' said Danny. He knew that everyone Julian came across was, either bribed, employed or disappeared. Except, that is, Peter. Although he had become one of them he was now most certainly on the side of law and order.

They came into Puerto Banus and Julian turned Paradise and moored up stern first.

'Now Danny bring some chilled champagne to the stern deck. We are free men and tomorrow we must go fishing. We must not keep the customers waiting too long'.

CHAPTER 37

Peter and Manuel sat in the rustic kitchen and drank red wine from the pitcher.

'He is going to pick up the drugs soon'. 'How do you know that someone else has not already done that?'

'If they have then we have lost. I think it's more likely they have hidden them'.

'That paravane could be anywhere by now'.

'I don't think so. Its range is probably very limited from the remote control. Manuel, I intend to get Julian in possession of his drugs and if necessary we will get past his corrupt Police friends and bring him to justice'.

'I think Skipper will help us, half his Police force is dead'.

'Ring him again and get him up here if you can'.

A short time later Skipper arrived in casual clothes. 'Yes I can help organise this for you but I cannot take part'.

Peter asked 'Is there a security firm I can get some help from? Preferably English, no offence, but I don't speak much Spanish'.

'You should learn another language, it is very useful' said Manuel.

Peter smiled at the dry humour returning to Manuel. 'Also we will require a helicopter'.

Skipper said 'Not a Police one I hope'. Skipper rang the security firm owner and he agreed to meet them in Marbella at his office within the hour.

Peter and Manuel walked swiftly up the stairs to the door marked 'Securiti Espana' and knocked. The door was opened by an Englishman of Peter's height, well-built and blond crew cut. His dark blue slacks and white open necked short sleeved shirt looking crisp and clean. His handshake was firm and dry. He looked up at Manuel who filled the doorway and offered his giant hand.

'Are you sure you need security?' he asked Peter with a smile. 'My name is Mike Evans. How can I help you?'

He listened to Peter's story without interruption. When Peter stopped he said 'The Senior Policeman you refer to is on the take with several known drug runners. I don't think I can help you with him. He could close us down with a phone call'.

Manuel spoke 'It's not him we want, its Julian'. Peter's face showed his attention had wandered. The policeman at the door back home, the hospital bed with his wife he could not wake, the boys that Julian had threatened.

Mike spoke 'Are you all right Peter?' He pulled up a chair and produced a small bottle of Chivas Regal from a cabinet. Pouring quickly he passed a glass to Peter.

Peter put his hand around the glass and looked at the bottle.

Mike said 'I know this Julian. I don't think he would hurt anyone'. The hand round the glass tightened until his knuckles were white. The glass exploded and blood began to seep from little cuts in Peter's hand. 'You are wrong' said Peter.

He recovered quickly and while wrapping his handkerchief around his hand said 'I want a surveillance team at points along the coast in touch by radio. I want you to monitor the yacht as it leaves Puerto Banus. Do nothing until the yacht stops offshore, which I think will be past Marbella Harbour. When she stops we expect two men to dive off. At that moment call us and we will be ready to take off by helicopter'.

'Do you need my men with you?'

'No' replied Peter. 'But can you supply automatic weapons and grenades?'

Mike said 'Yes'. He went on to say 'You are asking a great deal of me. The surveillance and reporting is not a problem, But I would not want guns and grenades traced back to me. I will also have to lease a helicopter'. He looked worried.

Peter chuckled 'Leave the hire of guns off the invoice'.

Manuel spoke for the first time 'Make sure the insurance is up to date on the helicopter'. This time Mike poured himself a drink. Peter looked again at the Chivas Regal "I see you know your whisky".

Peter and Manuel drove back to the farm. 'Manuel I would like to phone the UK and check on the family and also I think I should try and relay events to date in case something happens to me. I will pay for the calls'. Manuel replied in an authoritative voice that Peter had not heard before 'Yes you must speak to your family but I am insulted that you wish to pay me. I thought we were friends. As for something happening to you - I will be alongside you and that will make it difficult for them'.

Peter put his hand on the bulging muscle of Manuel's arm 'No offence meant, sorry Manuel'.

Peter dialled the hospital first. 'Your wife continues to remain in a stable condition. However, one of your sons swears that while he was sat with her yesterday, holding her hand, she squeezed it very slightly. We are afraid that he imagined it, as there is nothing to tell us that she has moved nearer to consciousness. Still it will encourage them to keep coming to see her'.

'Thank you' said Peter.

Next he phoned the school. The housemaster fetched Thomas. 'How are you son?'

'We are fine Dad. Josh's around the school somewhere. I've joined the cross country running team and Josh is in the rugby team'. He quickly spoke of the progress they were making at school and gave Peter a general update. 'Did you know that Mum squeezed Josh's hand?'

'Yes the nurse told me. Do you think she did?'

'Josh's positive she did, so that means she's going to get better Dad'.

Peter did not have the heart to dampen his enthusiasm. 'When are you coming home Dad?'

'Soon, but I want you to do something for me meanwhile. Tell Mummy this, that is whisper in her ear, I have found the man responsible for her car crash and he is a major criminal. I intend to bring him to justice. Tell her to hang on to that thought'.

'I thought you said you were a building manager in Spain'.

'I did, but you boys didn't believe that did you?'

'No Dad, we didn't. We also knew you would not tell us anything. We are grown up now, so, what is going on?'

'You would not believe me if I told you. I promise I will tell all eventually'.

'But why tell Mum this?'

'To give her something to fight for, son. Don't let her give up'.

'Come on Dad, Mum won't give up, she's as stubborn as you!'

Peter swallowed hard and blinked rapidly, 'Give my love to Josh'.

Manuel knew if he put his arm round Peter now they would both end up in tears.

Instead he went to attempt to make a cup of tea, which these English insisted on drinking. He did not possess a teapot but put the tea bags Peter had given him in the cups.

Peter then rang his old friend Chris and rapidly recounted his story. He asked Chris to make a note of the people's names, he knew to be criminals, and all information that would help bring them to justice. This included, especially, the Senior Officer of the Marbella police without whom Julian, Tony and Danny would still be in custody.

He knew that without extradition and with the corruption in the Police force it was going to be difficult to bring charges locally, if not impossible.

He asked Chris 'Do you have any news for me from your end?'

'Not really, when I saw the news on television that a Porsche went up in flames in London I wondered if it was the one you drove. They mentioned a couple of days later that the chap who was in hospital as a result of the explosion, whom the Police wanted to interview, had died'.

What he did not know was that a post mortem had shown the presence of poison in the bloodstream.

The Doctor passed the information to the police and so far neither police nor hospital could ascertain how this was administered.

CHAPTER 38

Mike Evans put together his surveillance team at intervals from Puerto Banus along the coast at 3 mile intervals, to Marbella Harbour mouth and 6 miles beyond. He arranged for two men at each position with both day and night binoculars and walkie talkies for communication.

Each man had rations and water. He rented a four man helicopter and held it on standby at a friend's villa just outside Marbella on the Antequara road. He also arranged for Peter and Manuel to wait there with him.

The owner of the villa was about to go away for a few days and was pleased at the thought of free security. He diplomatically did not ask what was going on and Peter smiled to himself at the way people just accepted suspicious goings on in this part of Spain.

Peter checked the arrangements with Mike and realised that Mike was a professional.

'What did you do before the Security business Mike?'

'Oh I was in the forces'. 'So was I, what did you do?' 'Much the same as I do now. Work behind enemy lines, so to speak'. 'You don't give much away Mike'.

'Sorry it's part of my training. I was in the SAS'.

Peter said. 'Perhaps we have met before!' They looked at each other with renewed interest.

'Maybe we should have reunions'.

'Nobody would say much' Mike replied.

As evening came, activity started on Paradise. Six men joined the others and immediately went below to the Stateroom. The six men, all Spanish, wore black jeans and black T-shirts. A mean looking bunch of thugs. Several had scars on face and arms. Each one was used to automatic machine pistols. Danny passed each one a bottle of San Miguel beer. Treating this as a signal to relax, one produced a packet of cigarettes and put one to his lips. Tony spoke 'This yacht is all No Smoking'. The Spaniard looked defiantly at Tony. Tony looked carefully along the sights of his pistols as if checking them. Then pointed the gun at the chandelier. 'No Smoking please' he repeated quietly. The Spaniard put the cigarette away and the tension in the room relaxed.

Julian said 'I thought my chandelier was a goner then, Tony'.

'Only on your orders boss'.

Julian said 'This is the plan. We put to sea shortly and will reach a location that I have memorised. We will be anchored for a little while during darkness and during that time you will be on guard against any visitors'.

He proceeded to show them the gun slots in the sides of the yacht. 'Two of you remain on deck but out of sight. The only bad luck would be a police patrol boat approach. Tony will do the talking. Danny and I will be doing a salvage operation'.

Some of the Spaniards did not speak English too well and there was some chattering amongst them. However, the pay was good and they did not mind what they did for it.

Paradise eased out of her moorings and Julian looked astern. He saw the gaping hole where the mooring post was torn out. Smiling he tried to picture Peter's face when he learnt that Julian had been released from prison. I expect he's on a plane now. It was all too much for our little family man, he thought to himself.

Although; it was out of character when he hit Tony. That was a professional at work. I wonder what his background was? His attention returned to navigating out of Puerto Banus.

The Spanish gunmen sprawled around the Stateroom beneath his feet and he could smell their presence. The distaste showed on his face. As he reached the little harbour entrance and turned towards Marbella the first surveillance man flicked a switch on his walkie-talkie. 'Subject leaving. Proceeding towards No 2'. Mike sat with Peter and Manuel holding an open frequency transmitter in front of them.

'You can relax for a while now' he said as the disjointed voice spoke.

Manuel said 'Shall I make a cup of tea?' Peter interjected as quickly as he could.

'No Manuel I'll do it. It's no trouble'. Mike and Peter spent quite some time trying to explain the theory of the tea making ritual. Manuel listened attentively but they were not convinced.

Mike said 'I will get you to the yacht but you can expect them to be ready for trouble.

By the way, I am coming with you'.

'Do you enjoy danger then?'

'No, I'm worried about all my equipment .'

'Number 2 reporting, subject proceeding as predicted'.

Peter and Manuel dozed on the couch. Mike and the helicopter pilot were playing cards in the dimmed lights of the villa. The pilot, concerned for his company profits, said 'This must be costing your client a fortune - can he pay'?

Mike said 'He has paid a substantial amount up front in cash so don't worry'.

'Another drug dealer is he?'

'Quite the opposite' Mike replied.

The hours ticked away and the surveillance team reported progress. Paradise, not showing navigation lights cruised on, slipping through the dark water with deceptive ease.

Julian, his face reflecting the green shadowy lights of the instrument panel, tapped into the computer the fix he had taken on the paravane's position. He studied the screen and watched as his own position showed and the two blips came closer together. He reduced speed and as the two blips united on the screen he stopped engines.

CHAPTER 39

Danny and Tony, posted as look outs on deck with the gunmen, could see no ships or boats in the vicinity.

Julian checked the depth beneath the keel, pressed a switch, and the anchor chain ran out. He called to Tony 'Don't trust these Spanish trigger happy slaves too much. But put them on alert. Any trouble, drop a grenade over the stern, we will feel it. If there is a hitch we will get to shore as before'.

Paradise rolled gently on the dark green swell as Julian and Danny put on their diving gear. Danny knew that he had no option but to co-operate fully with Julian and they both stepped off the stern platform and trod water, making their final adjustments to the breathing gear. Together they slid beneath the waves.

The final look out called into base 'This is Number 4 reporting. Subject has stopped. Position is 40 degrees to my right, 70 metres out'. They had all arranged with Mike that no grid references would be used in case they were overheard. This way only Mike could calculate their position.

Mike plotted the position on a map spread on the dining table. Little crosses marked the surveillance points and Mike drew a line from No. 4 position at 40 degrees. He measured 70 metres to scale and put another cross in the sea.

'Crude but it works' said Mike. 'I suggest we take the helicopter close to the shoreline without being seen, keep the engine running and when Number 4 spots any activity we move in'.

Peter spoke, 'If we do that he will jettison the paravane and we lose our proof. Could you take me out seaward of the yacht and drop me in the water without using your lights? 'The pilot nodded. 'Mike, do you have diving gear for me?'

'Yes I do, but I don't know what you are planning'. Peter rapidly gave his idea to Mike and Mike produced the equipment from his stores.

'Get the chopper started. I'll tell you as we fly'. The four of them jumped into the helicopter, passing the gear to each other and the rotors started their slow swirling into life. The pilot made his rapid checks and even as he did so Peter was peeling off his clothes in the cramped cockpit. The pilot took off, his navigation lights flashing steadily.

He headed for the shoreline and followed it in the direction of Marbella. Manuel, petrified at the experience of flying in the helicopter, was receiving rapid instructions for firing a machine pistol and use of grenades. Next, Mike turned his attention to Peter.

'Put on the hood and gloves, Peter, that water will be colder than you think'. Peter obeyed and strapped on the other tools and equipment Mike had produced. 'Any more and you will sink' shouted Manuel.

The pilot turned off all lights and turned the helicopter out to sea. The dull glow of the instrument lights cast shadows on their faces as the pilot flew only by his compass bearings. He came low to the water and skilfully skimmed the waves, shouting to Peter 'I will hover in the position I gave you. When you hit the water follow the course I showed you with your compass. We have tried to allow for the current but you will have some searching to do'.

Tony was called on deck and could hear the clatter of helicopter engines and scanned the area around the yacht with his night binoculars. He was not too worried, if it was the Police they would have searchlights and identity markings and navigation lights. He stayed on deck but the sound seemed all around him. He went below and checked the radar screen. There were a number of blips but nothing near the Paradise and nothing moving much. He returned to the bridge and settled in his chair sweeping the sea with his binoculars. He concluded someone else was up to no good.

The helicopter was almost touching the waves and Peter opened the sliding door.

Manuel put his hands under his shoulders and lowered him. They stayed for a second and Peter gave his thumbs up sign. The helicopter flew away to open sea and made a wide circle to the shoreline and switched on his lights. Mike spoke first 'All we can do now is wait. He has the best part of an hour's swim ahead of him'.

CHAPTER 40

Julian and Danny reached the beach and drew themselves wearily on the sand. 'I'm getting too old for this Danny'.

'It's all that high living' Danny replied. 'We are not fit'.

Julian drew a couple of whisky miniatures from his belt pouch and together they let the whisky flow and the warm glow spread from their stomachs.

'Once the shipment is made and we are paid, we can drop the dope dealing and go legit. You'd like that Danny, wouldn't you'.

'Yes, I would but I doubt if you could let go, it's so profitable and you enjoy the excitement'.

'I do but it's become a little too exciting, Danny'. They chatted while they rested and Danny felt the charisma of his boss envelop him as it always did. Julian found the rock formation he memorised to mark the spot and checked his compass. 'Come on Danny let's pick up the luggage'. They re-entered the water. They located the paravane and pulled the rocks from it. Julian operated the remote control and the paravane lifted magically from the sea-bed. It turned slowly in their torch beams and they grabbed a fin each.

Slowly and methodically Julian guided the paravane back to the yacht. As they came alongside Tony operated the winch and Danny clipped the hooks to the para-vane.

Julian and Danny swam to the steps and climbed aboard. Some of the hired gunmen idly watched the whole operation without comment.

Meanwhile, Peter swam blindly on through a well of darkness. The cold began to seep through the wetsuit. He maintained his regular breathing and slow methodical beat with his legs.

It was years since he had done any long distance underwater swimming and his legs were aching badly. He tried not to peer into the darkness but was aware of silver flashes of fish attracted by his torchlight. Checking the compass frequently and noting his time in the water he swam on.

Realising he was slower than they had all anticipated he continued for another 15 minutes. He could not see a ship's hull above him. I should have known better, this is impossible, he said to himself. It will be light soon and that will worsen my chances.

He headed slowly to the surface and raised his head, spinning his body in a circle. He saw the lights on land and continued turning, feeling like a periscope. 150 meters to his right he saw a dim silhouette. Submerging immediately he almost chuckled into his mouthpiece. I am fitter than I thought. I almost passed it by. He swam deeper in the direction of the yacht. He reached the anchor chain and held on to it.

On shore the Number 4 lookout had informed them that two men had left the yacht to swim ashore. So the question was, had they returned?

Peter saw the flashlight moving in the water towards the yacht! Had they spotted him? No, the paravane was in front and they were turning it towards the hull. He crouched motionless by the anchor, holding his breath, knowing his bubbles could give him away. The water was still dark and the 2 men concentrated on guiding the paravane to the surface. The torchlights disappeared and he assumed the paravane was being winched out of the sea and they were climbing aboard the yacht.

Peter went over the plan in his mind. He swam to the stern of the yacht and took a huge intake of air from his air bottles. Quickly slipping the harness off, he detached one air bottle, dived, and jammed it between the yachts propeller and the outer protecting ring.

Feeling the blood pounding in his temples and his lungs at bursting point he swam for the surface. Keeping close to the hull, he waited for his heaving chest and gasps for air, to come under control. Then he dived again and repeated the operation.

He surfaced and could hear Spanish being spoken on deck. As silently as he could, he swam along the length of the hull until he was directly beneath the paravane. It was out of reach as expected. Taking a deep breath he submerged vertically then thrust himself upwards. Scissoring his legs as fast as he could the fins pushed him up out of the water and he grabbed and held the rubbing rail on the side of the hull. He hung there by his fingertips.

Looking up he saw the guardrail of the deck. He began to swing fore and aft like a pendulum. The muscles of his shoulders creaked with the strain. His fingers rapidly lost any feeling.

With one mighty swing he released his right hand and reached up grabbing the lip of the deck. He reached higher and locked on with his left hand. He pulled himself up and rolled under the guardrail, exhausted.

Pulling a pair of wire cutters from his belt, he found the power feed to the winch operating the paravane crane. Quickly he cut through the cables to the motor.

Overcoming the desire to dive over the side he hung back over and lowered himself in stages into the water. Silently he swam to the stern. He knew that just above the bathing platform was a life belt and he cautiously lifted his head out of the water.

He could hear voices plainly now and knew someone could look over the stern at anytime. He pulled himself on to the platform and on his knees unhooked the lifebelt and its rope. He rolled off the bathing platform as a wave surged over it. Pulling his snorkel into his mouth he swam away from the yacht.

He tied the red flare to the belt and checked his watch. With only a few minutes to wait he held on to the life belt and paddled his legs slowly.

Paradise was rolling gently in the water and although he could see people moving around he could not recognise anyone.

The sound of the helicopter came gradually closer and Peter pulled the ring of the flare. With a rushing sound the sea and sky were lit up in a pink glow. Instantly Peter dived beneath the waves and put as much distance as he could from the floating firework.

Julian and his crew all rushed over and studied the flare. As they did so the helicopter came overhead and hovered. Mike called loudly through the loudhailer 'This is the Police. We know you have drugs aboard and we know you are armed. We should warn you that if you open fire we will sink you. Those are our orders'.

Julian thought for a moment. He turned to Danny and Tony 'Let's go below in case they start shooting anyway'. They ran quickly from the bridge.

'Start the engines and up anchor'.

Danny said 'What about the extra gun hands on deck?'

'Tough' Julian replied.

The helicopter hovered overhead and Peter trod water watching at a safe distance. He heard the Paradise engines start and prayed his jamming device would hold. Julian shoved the throttles forward again and again to no avail. Mike descended in the helicopter to a hailing distance. He switched on the searchlight. 'You now know we have disabled your yacht. Will you surrender and follow our instructions?'

Julian still in total command shouted 'Get up on deck and release the paravane'.

'Won't they ever learn? They won't have any proof'.

Danny and Tony ran up on deck and Tony hit the winch motor button 'Now what?'

Danny was down on his hands and knees looking at the severed cables. 'We can't shift that tin fish manually!' They ran back to Julian. 'We have saboteurs aboard, Julian'.

Mike yelled from the helicopter, 'Have you tried the paravane winch yet?' Manuel burst out laughing and the pilot grinned quietly to himself.

'Now all of you gather on the stern deck and let's see you throw all weapons over the side'. The powerful searchlight beam danced around the deck.

Julian issued his instructions and some extra ones to Tony. The gunmen and Danny and Julian all did as they were told.

Guns started splashing in the water all around the stern. The hired Spanish gunmen were looking very frightened with eyes casting round for means of escape. Julian stared thoughtfully at Danny.

Mike shouted to Manuel 'It seems to be working'. Then to the pilot 'Take us down'. As the helicopter came close, Tony appeared and at close range opened fire at the tail rotor first of all. He emptied the gun magazine as the helicopter roared out of control away from the yacht. It swooped and swayed desperately trying to gain height. Inside, Manuel was flung into Mike. The pilot still in his harness tried all he knew.

The body of the helicopter began to spin and they hit the water hard. Dazed, all three tried to open the doors but they were sinking quickly.

Julian gave a little wave to the helicopter as it sank from view. Water was pouring in. Manuel braced his shoulders against one side and put his feet to the door and pushed as hard as he could. He could not budge it. They were now underwater themselves and there was a pocket of air trapped under the roof of the cockpit. All three raised their faces and gulped the air down. The pilot, voice shaking, croaked 'I'm hit, you have only seconds left'. As he spoke the life was ebbing from him.

Peter dived down and down in the dark water guided by the cockpit lights of the helicopter. His teeth clamped firmly on the snorkel mouthpiece. Reaching the helicopter door he yanked quickly at the handle and the door swung open. They had not seen him and he slid up beside them and gasped for air. 'The door is open' he gasped 'take a deep breath and go'. He led Manuel out first knowing he was the most likely one to panic, but he didn't. He looked at the lifeless eyes of the pilot and knew he could do nothing for him. They headed for the surface and coughing and spluttering they looked over to the yacht.

Danny and Tony were both down in the engine room. 'I don't understand it.

Everything appears normal. It's like a giant hand is gripping the propellers'.

Julian stood behind them 'Someone on this boat is causing problems'. Danny spoke

'Don't look at me like that. I'm in this as deep as you are. What about the hired guns? Isn't that more likely? If you can get one to own up at least we will know what to do with the engines'.

The gunmen were milling around on the stern, some looking at the spot where the helicopter hit the water.

Julian approached them with Danny and Tony behind him. The hired gunmen no longer had their guns.

Julian shouted in Spanish 'One of you wrecked our engines. Step forward or I will shoot you one at a time'. No one moved. Julian gave a quick burst of fire and the nearest gunman was sent backwards into the rest 'Who's next?'

Danny knew if he tried to stop Julian it would be bad for him and Julian was in a mood to shoot anyone. Tony spoke 'Boss, if they know anything they would speak up now'. Julian opened fire again and another gunman died instantly.

Danny spoke 'This is getting us nowhere; tell them to jump overboard and head for the beach. That's what we are going to do'. The three of them began to argue amongst themselves.

CHAPTER 41

Silently, Peter climbed up the anchor chain and lay on the low deck. He reached down and pulled Manuel up beside him with Mike pushing from below. Mike climbed nimbly up and joined them.

Peter whispered his instructions 'Mike you take Danny, disarm him but keep him alive. Manuel take Tony, Mike will help you'. Manuel smiled 'That may not be necessary'.

Peter went on 'I want Julian for myself!

We have surprise as our only weapon. If they hear us coming we've had it'.

The three of them crept the length of the yacht. They slithered onto the roof of the cockpit area looking down on to the stern deck. Julian was shouting and waving his gun around. Tony had a hand on his arm trying to calm him down.

The three jumped down onto Julian and his men. Mike kicked the gun from Danny as he flew through the air. Manuel landed behind Tony and wrapped his arms around him in a bear hug.

Peter dropped onto Julian's back. The Spanish gunmen seeing their chance dived overboard in all directions.

Danny ran in low at Mike. Mike side stepped him and chopped his hand down in an expert karate blow. Danny, stunned and on his knees, groped for the gun. Mike kicked hard at Danny's head and knocked him out. Mike bent down and picked up the gun. As he did so Julian kicked him full in the face with Peter still hanging on his back wrestling with the gun.

Meanwhile Manuel squeezed Tony harder and harder with his hands pinned to his sides. Tony, well used to street fights, flicked the heel of his right foot up between Manuel's legs and the grip loosened. He pulled his arms free and stuck two straight fingers into Manuel's eyes. But Manuel was not finished, his bear hug was still holding. Tony kicked and gouged but slowly Manuel's strength was returning. Tony squirmed around in the grip until he was side on to Manuel. Manuel braced his legs and began to squeeze.

Tony was off the ground, his fists flailing. Manuel used his forearm to pull

Tony's ribs in. Tony's eyes were bulging, his breath cut off. Manuel, sweat and blood pouring down his face, used every ounce of power in his mighty frame.

Tony felt his ribs buckling. With a crack like a pistol shot, the bones snapped and stabbed into his lungs. Blood spurted from Tony's mouth as he collapsed lifeless.

Manuel threw him away like a rag doll, rubbing his eyes, trying to see where Peter was.

Julian smashed the gun into Manuel's head and he fell to the deck. Peter lay partly under him, blood oozing from the back of his head. Julian had lunged backwards with Peter on his back, smashing his head into the metal bulkhead.

In deathly silence Julian looked around him. The two Spanish gunmen lay dead.

Peter and Manuel lay senseless beside them. He turned to look for Mike and as he did so Mike swept his legs from under him. Julian fell but was cushioned by the huge bulk of Manuel. Mike, still groggy, reached for the machine pistol and threw it overboard. Julian, crazed by his loss of the gun, tore into Mike who was on his hands and knees.

With both feet he kicked Mike about the head and body until he moved no more.

Julian stood there, eyes wild, chest heaving and sweat pouring down his face. He gradually gained his composure and forced himself to think. He knew that reinforcements must appear soon. The yacht rocked gently in the swell and he looked to the shore lights. His mind made up he went below decks and rapidly climbed into his diving gear. He slipped quietly off the diving platform and settled into a leisurely swim towards the beach.

On deck Danny came to first and looked at the bodies. Tony, his pal with whom he had shared so much, was dead. Eyes wide open and a look of wild disbelief on his face. Peter was groaning, trying to push Manuel off him. Danny pulled Peter out from under Manuel and sat him up. Manuel stirred and grunted.

Mike was unconscious but breathing steadily. Danny went to the galley and drew a bucket of fresh water. He grabbed a bottle of whisky from the rack and returned to the others.

He sloshed water into Peter's face and Manuel's as well. They passed the bottle round. Danny spoke 'He's gone Peter. Tony's dead. Two Spanish gunmen dead. The rest are gone. That chap there is unconscious and looks as though he took a good kicking'.

'He's with us' Peter replied.

'So am I now'.

Peter looked steadily at Danny for a moment 'OK', he replied.

'This isn't over yet but we need to get Mike to a hospital and I guess Julian is headed back to shore anyway'.

Manuel said 'If he's swimming we may see him'.

'Don't mince him up with the propellers - he's mine'.

Peter said 'I will go over the side and free the propellers if I can'. He went below and grabbed some goggles. He slipped beneath the waves and the sea water stung the cut on the back of his head. The oxygen bottles were stuck firmly but he wrenched one free and headed for the surface with lungs bursting again.

As soon as he regained his breath he dived again and sent the other bottle to the seabed.

Peter shouted from the water 'Try that Danny'.

He only just managed to pull himself on to the bathing platform and lay there for a moment.

Danny started the engines and moved the throttles to 'slow ahead 'both'. Still no movement as Danny applied power. Manuel looked over the bow rail. 'Would it help to raise the anchor?'

They all laughed together and the tension lifted. They headed back to port and the yacht scythed through the waves sending the bow wave wide in front of them. A lone swimmer in black wet suit heard the engines and dived beneath the waves, not knowing if it was Paradise. He swam under water for a while, surfacing to see the dark silhouette in the distance.

Paradise slipped unobtrusively into Marbella and they took a visitors mooring near the harbour wall.

Peter spoke 'We must alert a hospital for Mike but we had better not stay around with two dead men on board'. Danny used the ship to shore radio 'Emergency - Motor Yacht Paradise calling - moored in the main harbour - we have an injured crewman- medical help required immediately'. The reply came 'Acknowledged - help is on the way'.

'Let's go'. Peter led the way.

They returned to the Nissan. Danny said 'I remember this truck' looking at the broken windscreen. 'It's a hire car isn't it?'

'One careful driver' Peter replied.

'Where to now?'

Manuel spoke up 'My farm'.

'I thought you'd never offer'.

Danny said 'First place Julian will look'.

'He won't be looking. He's gone to ground by now. Think about it. He knows we won't rest until we find him. Although the local Police are in his pocket, the proper authorities want him. And most of all he's one drug shipment adrift so someone's shouting for his blood. No, he won't look for us'.

CHAPTER 42

The only thing in the world that could scare Manuel stood at the door with her arms folded. Each one of them walked quickly past her. Dirty, bloodied, unshaven.

Out of character she put water on to boil without saying a word. Manuel said 'I will make English tea for us'.

'That's all I need' Peter replied. Danny looked puzzled.

As they cleaned themselves up they discussed the next move 'If we can find Julian we have enough evidence and witnesses to his killings to put him away for life'.

'Murder is a capital offence here' Danny said.

'Lawful execution is too good for him, Danny, you know him, where will he be?'

'He won't go to his villas, that's for sure. He would hide in a friend's house or someone who owes him a favour'.

'We'll get some rest, get cleaned up and start asking around'.

Much later they climbed back into the Nissan and drove into Puerto Banus. Using the big public car park behind the harbour Peter led the way on foot.

'When I first came here I spoke to a waiter who obviously knew Julian but wasn't telling me anything'.

'I know who that is' Danny replied. They walked into the restaurant and settled themselves on three bar stools. 'Hi Marco, seen Julian around?' Danny enquired.

Peter recognised him as the one who allowed him to shower and change previously.

'No, I am sorry, he has not been in lately'. They sat drinking their beer and Marco went out the back. 'He's phoning' Peter started off his stool but Manuel was quicker.

'Stay here'. Marco's jaw dropped as Manuel loomed over him. He lifted him bodily off his feet and threw him into a stack of cases of wine glasses - the phone still clenched in his hand ripped off the wall. Manuel stooped beside him and listened.

Danny and Peter heard the crash of glass but were not too worried. 'He remembered' stated Manuel. 'He'll tip him off now' said Danny.

'I don't think so, he seemed frightened of me, and anyway the phone does not work now'.

'We must drive to El Harvin le Grande. There is a certain restaurant he uses. Do you know it?' Peter thought for a moment 'Of course, the Alcutin'.

They headed out of Puerto Banus and into the hills. The little village was quiet and again they walked into the restaurant.

'No I have not seen him lately' said Pablo.

Manuel advanced towards him. As he did so there was a burst of gunfire and the sound of a car roaring off. They ran outside. The Nissan tilted at an angle as the air hissed out of a front tyre. Through the dust Peter thought he recognised a white Mercedes SL.

They went back in. 'I am surprised you did not know Julian was here ' said Manuel.

Pablo looked terrified. They would never catch up with him now.

Peter said 'I am hungry, what do you say to a meal on the house, while you think about this misunderstanding'. 'Yes, yes of course, anything'.

They ate their food as fast as it was placed in front of them, not noticing the high quality of the food and hardly touching the wine. Pablo hovered over them, nothing was too much trouble. 'Pablo do you have any idea where he might have gone?'

'No, Senor, but he told me he must leave Spain quickly'.

Peter spoke to the others 'If that's the case, I guess he will go to the villa he's just bought and pick up some cash and belongings'.

'Pablo, I want to ask you a favour'.

'Anything Senor'.

'What car do you drive?'

'Senor, she's my pride and joy, you wouldn't?'

Manuel stood up and stretched his arms, his great chest expanded and the muscles tightened like knotted rope. Pablo disappeared out the back entrance and the deep rumble of a sports exhaust came loud and clear through the restaurant. The red Ferrari arrived at the front door.

Pablo said 'She is not new but, how you say, a collection piece'.

Peter slid into the driver's seat and the centre boss of the steering wheel displayed the black prancing horse on yellow background. Peter gave rapid directions to Danny and Manuel for his villa.

'Change that wheel and catch me up'. He roared off down the road taking the bends with squealing tyres. 'Change down, slow into the corner, foot to the floor and accelerate out' he said to himself as his spirits lifted.

He quickly covered the distance and turned into the opulent residential district. He stopped the Ferrari short of the big black gates of the villa. Making up his mind he reversed a little and put the car out of sight. Avoiding the gates for fear of cameras he climbed the railings and dropped quietly into the bushes. Still, for a moment, he just listened, no dogs, no alarms just the chirrup of cicadas.

The brilliant bougainvillea and hibiscus filled his nostrils. Using the bushes for cover he followed the driveway to the pillared entrance. He paused, all was quiet. Turning, he followed the wall of the house around and came upon the patio by the swimming pool.

Julian sat at the table calm and composed. 'I've been expecting you'. His hand was resting gently on a Walther PPK pistol.

CHAPTER 43

'Sit down Peter'. Peter walked over to the table forcing the tension out of his body.

'All this was so unnecessary. I gave you a good time and money. A chance to build a new life. But no, not you, with your principles and morals'.

Peter sat there, face white, seething, fighting for control.

'You murderer, you sick drug peddling pervert'.

Julian unmoved replied 'I am the one with the gun, remember'.

'So what happens now?'

'Because of you I need to leave Spain and that means leaving a lot behind which hurts.' I have loaded the Merc with more cash than you'll see in a lifetime. But I am still ahead'.

'Ahead of what? Are you happy? Do you have a wife and kids who love you? You have nothing compared to me'. Little beads of perspiration were appearing on

Julian's brow. A little twitch started at the corner of his mouth.

Peter sensed he was getting through but knew he risked being shot. He changed tack.

'What do you want me to do?'

'I want you to die, Peter. But I want to watch it happen. I want you to start pleading with me. Don't worry; I won't shoot unless I have to. Here snap this on your wrist'.

A pair of handcuffs lay on the table. At gun point Peter did as he was told.

As he lifted his hand he realised he was handcuffed to the heavy wrought iron table.

'You enjoyed the pool didn't you Peter. Well you are going swimming again. Drag that table to the edge'.

Peter did not move. 'Do it or I'll shoot your knee caps and drag you myself'.

Peter's mind raced ahead. How long would he have? Two minutes? Could he break the handcuffs? Or the table? Could he drag it? One thing's for sure, if I don't do it I am dead. He dragged the heavy table to the pool edge. Julian, smiling now, stood beside him.

'I figured it out, you know, you jammed my propellers. That's what made me think of it. You like going under water'.

Still with gun in hand he shoved the table hard and with a great splash Peter had no choice but to go with it. As the bubbles cleared he could see Julian at the poolside. His white teeth showed as he laughed. Peter had taken a huge gulp of air as he went in.

He began to tug the handcuffs harder and harder. It was hopeless. He held his breath for as long as possible. He began to release air in a trickle to buy more time.

He did not take his eyes off Julian.

He became light headed. A picture of Jane flashed before him. Golden hair, laughing, running with the two boys. He began to choke. His lips parted, water rushed in. All quiet, peaceful even, darkness descended. Julian bored by the anti climax, shrugged, and walked quickly around the house to the Mercedes. He drove swiftly down the drive.

The big Nissan charged at the black gates, the security locks hardly checking its speed. Danny instinctively put his hand in front of his face. Through the gates Manuel saw the Mercedes and swerved automatically. Julian sped through the gates and was gone.

Danny shouted 'Peter wasn't with him'.

' We are too late' Manuel said.

They screeched to a halt in front of the house. The Spanish maid was there, screaming and shouting. Manuel followed her around to the pool, with Danny at their heels.

Manuel did not pause in his run. He plunged into the pool and swam beneath the table. Danny catching on fast was beside him. They dragged the limp body onto the table.

Manuel positioned himself between the legs of the table and stood up. Peter rose above the water, spread on the table. Manuel stood like Colossus. His legs were like trees straining with the weight. He locked his knees and head still under water he strode slowly to the pool ladder. Danny was ahead of him. From the ladder he tried to take some of the weight. Using one hand Manuel began to pull his way up. A blood red mist in front of his eyes. His head spinning. His lungs screaming for air.

One foot touched the bottom rung. His head broke the surface. He gulped air and kept on climbing. Danny and the girl pulled from above. Manuel heaved the table and Peter onto the paved area and sank to all fours. Danny tipped the table on its side. Peter rolled on to his back. Danny tipped the head back and began resuscitation. He prayed as he pushed hard on the sternum of the chest. He pinched the nostrils and blew air into the water filled lungs. Manuel, recovering his own breath, shouted

'Peter don't give up'. Danny worked away. A movement, a splutter, water gushed from Peter. Coughing and heaving he returned from the dead.

CHAPTER 44

The maid went to the house and returned with an axe. One swift motion and Peter was severed from the table. Peter spoke 'No wise cracks please Manuel. I am not in the mood'.

'I am too tired' Manuel replied.

They stood Peter up and walked him towards the house.

At each step Peter's head cleared a little. 'I think he's headed for the yacht'.

'Leave it to the Police now Peter'.

He broke away from them, running on legs made of rubber. Out of the gates he jumped into the Ferrari. Danny was close on his heels and pulled him out.

'You're not fit to drive. Get in the other side. Manuel bring the truck. Alert your friends. The Police won't stop Julian'.

Manuel turned and sprinted back. Danny gunned the Ferrari in a tight circle leaving black rubber on the road. Peter thought he could drive but this was something else!

The Ferrari streaked down the hill with Danny heel and toeing on the pedals. He picked up the main road to Marbella. Traffic in both directions. Danny maintained speed anyhow he could. Trucks blasted horns and flashed lights. Cars darted out of his path. He passed either side, through the red lights, and, where traffic stopped he went up on the pavement. A flashing blue light fell in behind them but could not keep up. They roared on to the harbour wall. The Mercedes was there. Jumping out of the car they ran to the end of the wall. Paradise was moving out of the harbour. They glanced down but the yacht was four meters down and too far from the wall to jump the gap.

'Danny, get a boat quick'. Danny fell for the trick, running back. Peter watched the yacht turn the corner of the wall. Going back a few paces he sprinted to the end. He launched himself into the air as Paradise gained speed. A perfect landing on all fours onto the roof of the bridge.

Julian, handling the boat alone, guessed someone unwelcome had arrived. He picked up the Walther PPK and started firing above his head. Peter rolled clear and counted. Six shots and click. The unmistakable sound of a hammer on an empty chamber. Peter swung down off the canopy in a somersault and kicked out at Julian.

Half turned towards him Julian took the kick in the arm. Peter was upon him. His hands went for the throat. He was ready for the head butt and jerked his own head back. Ready again for the knee to the groin he moved side on. The knee deflected on his own leg. Relentlessly he increased pressure on the throat. Julian, punching and gouging, began to weaken. His body sagged. Peter fell for it. Julian broke free and hit the throttles with his elbow. The mighty diesels responded and Peter was thrown off balance. Julian was upon him but this time the odds were even. No weapons, no help. Peter, calling on his combat training and natural strength and agility, Julian using animal cunning, desperate, scrabbled for a hold. The yacht now surging ahead on full power towards the open sea. Peter wriggled out from beneath Julian and he got to his feet. Julian rushed in low. Peter, with his weight on his forward foot, brought his fist up in a classic upper cut. He felt the teeth snap off at the gums.

Julian went backwards, straightened up by the blow. This time Peter kicked and found his target. The soft flesh yielded beneath his foot. Julian crumpled. Peter pulled him to his feet. He drove his head butt into the already damaged face.

The bridge of the nose snapped. Barely conscious now Peter used him like a punch bag. He drove his fist into the solar plexus. Julian bent over. Peter punched repeatedly. He let him drop to his knees. Grabbing Julian's hair he looked at the damage to his face. Surprised by the mess he had made he held him there.

Julian smiled through toothless gums, blood running from nose and mouth. 'Your wife died a few days ago. I forgot to tell you'.

Goaded to a new fury he dragged Julian to his feet. He twisted the arm up behind the back until Julian screamed. He ran him into the superstructure headfirst again and again. Blood trickled from both ears.

Disgusted, Peter threw him into the corner of the cockpit. He landed in a sitting position. Peter saw the eyes staring straight ahead. He kicked out with all his remaining strength and Julian slumped to the deck. Those already lifeless eyes now squashed.

Peter, sickened by his own actions, turned his back on him and reached for the throttles bringing the yacht to a slow stop. He hit the drop anchor button and slumped over the wheel. Head on his arms, he cried.

He cried for his wife, he cried for his own actions and he cried from sheer exhaustion. Some time later he threw a bed sheet over Julian and went below to the Stateroom. Pulling a bottle from the silver gimbal, he poured Remy Martin into a crystal glass.

I should have kept in touch. How are the boys managing? Like it or not I've committed murder. If I take the yacht in, the Police will be waiting for me. If I tip him over the side, someone will find the body. I've got to get home. The thoughts ran through his head. He poured another brandy. For the first time he spotted the suitcases thrown down in a hurry. He unlocked both. Each case had the same contents. Stuffed full of Euros. Large denomination used notes. Hundreds of thousands of pounds worth. Instinctively he put them in a locker.

The brandy flowed over him. The sofa felt so comfortable. Sleep beckoned him. Julian's eyes stared at him. He was anchored at the bottom of the pool. A red Ferrari flew by. Handcuffs. An axe. His imagination ran riot in his nightmare. He woke with a jolt.

Inevitable I suppose, the police are here. There is no way out. It was a fair fight.

CHAPTER 45

A voice called out. The deep boom of Manuel. The higher pitch of Danny. 'Down here' he called.

Both men appeared 'We thought that was you under a sheet on the bridge. You just had to finish it alone, didn't you'.

The reprimand stung. 'Yes I did!'

'Well looking at the mess he's in; remind me not to upset you'.

Peter poured them both a brandy.

'We have a boat alongside' Danny said. He took charge. He knew Peter was deeply troubled by the fight. 'This yacht can stay here. The police won't be too concerned by the death of a murdering drug peddler. Don't forget he killed police amongst others. Let's go'.

Peter perked up 'I want to bring a couple of suitcases'.

'It looks like you need a change of clothes' quipped Manuel.

Danny watched Manuel and Peter board the other boat. He called out 'Give me a moment'. He grabbed the corpse of his former boss by the ankles and dragged him down the steps in to the stateroom. Julian's head bumped down the steps. Taking a couple of bottles of the Remy Martin he sloshed it over the sumptuous Chinese rugs. Next, he went below to the engine room. There he opened the sea-cocks.

Returning to the stateroom he took a silver cigarette lighter that he had never seen used. He lit the brandy soaked rug and watched the flames take hold. They left the Paradise drifting, already lower in the water and started motoring back to harbour. Peter stood on the stern deck and watched as Paradise became engulfed in flames. His last memory of that yacht was as she slid beneath the waves in a shroud of steam.

Danny spoke, 'Don't worry; there won't be a reception committee. All will go quiet now. The police in Julian's pay will keep a low profile and the file on him will disappear. His contacts in London and here will just cut their losses and set up new contacts. Some people will get caught and punished and some will get away. But for you it's over' Danny consoled him.

'My wife died and I wasn't there, how do you think that makes me feel?'

'How do you know she's dead?'

'Julian blurted it out in the fight'. 'Get me to a phone'.

Manuel and Danny took turns at the wheel and left Peter to his depression. Just as Danny anticipated there was no reception committee in the harbour. They tied up and returned to the cars taking the suitcases with them. They drove out of the harbour area and stopped at a small hotel.

Peter walked into reception. 'I need to use a phone in private' and he put down a Euro note. 'Can you help me?'

The receptionist pointed to a booth and quickly folded the note into her palm. The phone call bounced off the satellite and rang in the hospital reception.

'All I can tell you is there is no one here of that name'.

'Where is she?'

'Look we don't give much information on the phone'.

'I am her husband!'

'Yeah' said the receptionist. 'There is no one around to help and I have another

255

call, sorry'. The line went dead. He could not bring himself to ring the boys.

Sensing the gloom Manuel said 'The best thing you can do is get a flight tomorrow and go home'.

They stopped at a travel agent and booked a flight at 12 noon for the next day.

Walking out of the hotel they saw two uniformed police examining the Ferrari. 'Don't panic, they probably saw it being driven quickly' Danny said. They walked past it and climbed into the Nissan. 'I think it would be wise to lay low until your flight. We will go back towards Puerto Banus and join the tourists'.

Danny knew a hotel owner who would not ask questions or talk and he paid the man handsomely from the suitcase for his discretion. They put Peter in with Danny and Manuel had a room to himself. Peter was saying very little and Danny filled the bath and encouraged Peter to have a soak.

He noticed the cuts and bruises over Peter's body. He had forgotten just how much Peter had been through. Later, Peter, his muscles stiffening up, attempted to get out of the bath but Danny had to help. He put a towel round his shoulders and Peter yelped with pain.

He quickly fetched Manuel 'I don't want to do this without a witness'. Taking the hair dryer he began to dry Peter with the hot air. Peter stood like a dog having a shampoo, head hung down. Between them they put him to bed and Manuel returned to his room with two suitcases beside him. Danny lodged a chair under the door handle of their bedroom, just in case.

The next morning Peter, though very stiff, felt better and the three of them had a light breakfast and walked in to the Puerto Banus boutiques and bought some new clothes.

Danny said 'How do you want to spend your last few hours?' Peter walked them back round to the harbour and sat on a seat overlooking the yachts.

They sat each side of him and then he spoke. 'I came here to get Julian, I wanted him to stand trial but it all got out of hand'. He paused. 'A lot of people have helped me and I want you to see that those people get some cash'.

'Like who?'

'How about people at the Nissan hire company? I won't be too popular there.

Then there's Mike and the helicopter pilot. I need to know if that pilot had family. Pablo the Ferrari owner. You know, the list goes on. What about you two, I don't want the money'.

Manuel spoke 'I don't want drug money either'.

'You need a new tractor though'.

Manuel rubbed his formidable chin. 'Maybe'.

Danny said 'Are you going to turn me in'.

'I owe my life to you both. You are Treasurer, Danny, what's left, start a new life.'

'Come and see me, both of you'.

CHAPTER 46

Peter sat forward, his elbows on his knees and in the distance he idly watched a man pushing a woman in a wheel chair. Coming towards them he saw the two boys. One either side. The sun shone on the water, the reflection making it difficult to see their features. As they came closer he could see the golden hair of the woman. The two boys broke into a run. Peter was on his feet.

They practically bowled him over. With one boy on each hand he ran towards the wheelchair. Down on his knees he grabbed her hands and looked into her face. Jane smiled that smile. Chris let go of the wheel chair and put his hand on Peter's shoulder for a moment then walked towards Danny and Manuel.

'I am a friend of Peter's' he introduced himself.

'So are we' they replied in unison.

Diplomatically, Manuel, Danny and Chris withdrew to the bar of one of the restaurants nearby.

Jane's voice was slurring badly and she spoke haltingly so that the boys kept finishing her sentences for her. She showed her dismay for Peter's injuries and smiled lopsidedly as he brushed away the concern. Peter learnt that although she could not walk or lift her hands, all these symptoms would recede, but she had two years of treatment ahead.

He chose his moment to say 'The one that did this to you has been caught and faces the death sentence for murder'. 'Not strictly true as the punishment has already been handed out'. He said silently to himself.

The family reached a decision; they would like to stay on for a few days. Thomas fetched the other three from the bar. Chris said 'We brought a nurse with us to look after Jane. I sent her for an ice cream, she'll be back soon. She walked towards them as he spoke. Her tight blue jeans and striped T-shirt quivering, holding the men's attention.

Peter said 'How old is she?' 'About 23' Chris smiled. 'Is she a capable nurse?' 'I didn't ask' he joked. Peter knew very well that Chris would have chosen the best nurse available.

They all returned to the hotel and settled around a table by the pool. As the waiter brought the drinks Peter fingered the table and glanced at the pool. The nightmare returned, his heart thumped in his chest and the sweat began to run down his face.

Josh said 'You're still not used to the heat then Dad'. Chris spoke at just the right moment 'He usually puts a hanky on his head, when it's this hot'. Jane was watching. She spotted how Chris took the heat out of the moment. If she had not known Peter better she could have sworn she saw a tear mingle with the sweat. In vain she tried to lift her arm to comfort him, but it would not move.

She looked over at Manuel and Danny and saw the discomfort every time they moved. Stiff limbs, cuts and bruises. She hoped all would be explained but doubted if that would be the case.

Danny said to Chris 'Lets go to reception and get you booked in' 'Right I'll get the luggage. The two boys were given their own room. Danny and Manuel were to share Danny's existing room. They up-graded Peter and Jane to the best room in the hotel. Chris walked back over to the nurse. He said 'The hotel is fully booked now. They have one double room left. What do you think? It's only for one night. I must go home tomorrow and there is a sofa in the room'.

Chris did not move so much as an eye-lash, but his eyes seemed to twinkle even more than usual.

They all went to their rooms to rest and shower, agreeing to meet for dinner. Jane rested on the bed and Peter, restless, paced around the room. He looked out of the window and saw the boys standing on the diving board. One behind the other they ran and dive bombed in to the pool.

'I thought the boys were resting'. He said.

'They are more like young men now. They have been marvellous'. She replied. 'But you three move like old men. What's been going on Peter?' He paused for a moment,

'You know when I was on active service and people questioned me, I would duck out. Do you mind if I do that for now. We are together and you will get well, that's all that matters'. Jane just nodded, her eyes drooped and she dozed off. He realised that the journey and then trying to talk had tired her out.

In the early evening the party sat around the table for dinner. Chris had requested a table in the dining room, remembering how the pool seemed to upset Peter. Jane had lectured the boys on not asking too many questions. Peter said 'Do you mind if I order the food. I am sure you will all like it'. The waiter arrived 'We will start with Gazpacho followed by Rabo de toro a la rondena. Afterwards, do you have some Mancheyo cheeses for us to try? Although, my sons may prefer the Pestines. Could we have a few bottles of Marques de Alella, the '82 if possible'? The waiter lifted his eyebrows 'An excellent selection Senor'. 'Beer for the boys? 'Yes please'. They shouted in unison before Peter could speak.

Chris said 'You've learnt a bit about food while you've been here' 'It's been an eventful trip in many ways'. Peter replied, as he watched the nurse spoon feed Jane. As the evening progressed the friends made their plans. Manuel said he dare not stay away any longer and would return home tomorrow. Danny decided to go to Julian's villa and see if there was anything important there that could incriminate them. The maid would still be there and he would pay her off. Peter noted the underlying decency of the man again.

Chris spoke last 'I must fly back tomorrow; the nurse can stay with Jane and travel with you when you are ready'. They all agreed to keep in close touch in case anything unexpected happened. 'Chris, could we have a coffee together tomorrow morning, please'. Peter whispered.

The hotel was quiet in the early morning. They took their coffee out in to the gardens. Rapidly, Peter brought Chris up to date. 'My problem is, in England there is a warrant out for my arrest. I can't stay in Spain for long; there are questions the Spanish Police will want answered. It could take months to sort out. Could you find out the attitude of our Police to me if I return? I don't think I have done anything wrong'.

Chris probed 'You haven't told me what Julian did with the drugs. You said he collected them in Gibraltar. He brought them back to Spain, then what?' Peter walked over to reception and asked them to call

Danny to join them. They brought Danny up to speed on the conversation. 'Danny, do you know where the drugs went from here?'

'London, that's all I know'.

Chris promised to relay all this to Chief Superintendent Reynolds in the hope that he would agree to accept the part Peter had played if there was a chance of 'nailing Mr Big'. Chris said his goodbyes and Peter remained in his debt for bringing Jane and the boys to him.

'How did you find me?' Chris smiled, shook hands and left.

Peter turned to Danny ' Did Julian ever phone his connections in the U.K.?

'I think so'.

'In the booths, from his yacht or villa, or his mobile'.

'Slow down Peter, what are you thinking?

'We could trace his calls'. 'Impossible, you know how tight lipped the local Police are'. Peter finally said 'We will ask Manuel to get his Police friends to help'.

CHAPTER 47

That morning the family moved in to holiday mode. The nurse played in the pool with the boys. Peter and Jane sat nearby sipping their drinks, Peter holding the glass for Jane as she sucked through a straw.

A few days went by before Manuel came to see Peter. 'I have the information on some of the phone calls. The local Police have talked to your Police and we have some addresses. One call he often made was to someone called Barney who they say has died. He called one or two acquaintances whom your Police say are probably not involved. There is a London firm of lawyers who confirm they have acted for him on a property transaction. They are not keen to give details'.

Peter asked 'What about the last ten days? Let me look at the printouts'. The number of calls diminished, he noticed. He backtracked in his mind to when he read in the paper that the Porsche had been blown up in London. 'That was about the sixteenth, I think' On the seventeenth Julian had made a phone call from to a London number. 'Could this be the connection?' He folded the printout and put it in his pocket. The two friends parted and Peter returned to his family.

Nothing happened for a couple of days until Chris phoned. 'I have spoken to the Police and they asked me to meet Superintendent Reynolds. Apparently, he has been digging in to your past. He would not give any details but grudgingly stated he has a new respect for you. He said what has happened in Spain does not interest him.

He felt it necessary to point out that it is possible he may have to arrest you on your return to the UK. He could possibly try and charge you with involvement with drug trafficking and murder but it doesn't seem to be uppermost in his mind... He does not see Julian's death as any great loss. He feels the law would be better served by finding the London connection. Don't forget, British Police officers were killed and injured at the warehouse raid in Fulham'

Peter said 'On that basis we will return home in the next few days. See you soon'.

Peter returned to the hotel room and explained to Jane that when they arrived home he would be helping the Police, and he released a little information regarding Julian's activities.

He looked out of the window and saw the boys in the pool. 'It's time to slay the dragon'. He said to himself. He put on his shorts and made for the pool.

'We'll race you Dad' Thomas shouted on seeing him.

'Give me a day or two to get fit' he replied.

'Dad, you're covered in cuts and bruises. You'd better sit by the pool and watch us'.

Peter sat there bringing the demons under control. Suddenly, he stood up, dived in and swam a length under water. He got out quickly and returned to his room. Jane had watched, puzzled.

On the Saturday they flew back to Bristol. The nurse supervising Jane, and the airline staff giving her every attention. They all squeezed in to Peter's car and drove back to Bath. Peter learned that Jane should not have been released from hospital so soon but had discharged herself. She had guessed something was going on. She had lain for days in the hospital fully aware of what was going on around her before she could move or speak. Finally she had asked the boys to bring Chris to the hospital.

He knew Manuel's' mobile number as Peter had given it to him in case anything happened to him. They also knew that Peter would not have agreed to Jane travelling.

What they did not know was that he had been told she was dead. Chris had telephoned Manuel and it was decided they would travel to the hotel and Manuel would keep the secret just that bit longer. They knew Peter would only believe she was OK if he saw her himself.

Once they were home and settled in, Peter phoned the hospital.

'I know it's Saturday but is Dr Wylies on duty?

'Yes he is'. He came to the telephone and was pleased that Jane was back. He said 'I have never seen such determination in anyone. Well, Peter, that is to say, almost anyone'.

He had never called him Peter before. He recommended that Jane should attend physiotherapy but there was no need to stay at the hospital.

The nurse was sitting with Jane in the living room and Peter went to them 'Nurse, would you be willing to live in with us and take Jane to the hospital and look after her here?'

'Yes I would, on one condition', Peter waited, 'Call me Sue, not nurse'.

'Great Sue, you're one of the family. I'll be generous, don't worry'.

He went to the study and phoned his Manager. 'Can you come to the house in the morning, Ron, and fill me in on business?'

'Certainly'. Ron turned up at ten thirty, prompt as always. Peter listened to progress and saw there was no cause for concern.

'Ron, you are running this business on your own these days. I am going to make you director and give you a shareholding'.

'Thank you, boss, just as long as I know you are there if I need you'. He knew Peter would be fair with him.

Sue said she would be happy to take the boys to and from school on her way to the hospital with Jane. The boys would have been happy to board but Jane wanted to feel they were coming home each day with their news.

Peter decided to give Sue his car to use, and made a few calls to garages. Some were indifferent to his call. If they only knew him better. He had been shown more enthusiasm, in Spain, when buying a sandwich. When he rang the BMW dealer the salesman said he had a 325CI Coupe that seemed to fit the bill.

'Could you bring it round?' Within the half hour it was on the driveway. It was only a few months old. 'I don't like haggling so tell me your best price'.

The salesman looked at the battered face with the air of authority about it. '£20,000 if you say yes now'. Peter sat down and wrote out the cheque. 'When can I have it?'

'Now, if you give me a lift back to the showroom. But don't you want to try it?'

'It's all right isn't it?'

Well, of course, and if I may say so sir, I would not like to be the man to sell you something that you were unhappy with'.

Peter looked puzzled and said 'Let's go'.

On the way back from the showroom he thought 'That's the domestics sorted out'.

When he got home he phoned the Police and asked for an appointment with Superintendent Reynolds for Monday morning. He enjoyed his family Sunday and helped Sue cook lunch.

CHAPTER 48

Monday morning at 9 a.m. he sat opposite C.S.Reynolds. The unsmiling Senior Police Officer looked at his battered face and hands. 'Now Haynes' he started.

'Hold it right there' Peter cut in 'You can call me Peter or Mr Haynes if you must, but I don't like Haynes'. It had the desired effect and startled Reynolds. Peter went on 'I know you like to stamp your authority on people but I am happy to help all I can and it is not necessary with me'.

Reynolds recovered and sensed the inner strength of the man. He leaned forward towards Peter using the body language to convey friendliness. 'Well, Peter, tell me what you know'. They talked for two hours and Reynolds made copious notes.

Reynolds said 'We are agreed that someone well informed and connected, probably based in London, masterminds the whole thing'.

'That's near enough but I doubt if he has anything to do with the original source. They seem to compartmentalise the transactions'.

Reynolds replied 'I appreciate that, but we think that the connection in London is the one who organises distribution. If we get him we will get them all'.

Peter said 'I have a phone number which may be all you need'. He pulled the printout from his pocket. 'We have discounted the other numbers and this one seems most likely'.

Reynolds stood up to tell someone to trace the number. Peter said 'One sugar, please'.

As Reynolds left the room he actually smiled and said 'Don't push it too far' He returned with two mugs of tea and said 'I have had the number traced and a good job I did. That is a private line to the Chairman of the Mercantile and Colonial Bank in the City. That is Sir John Miles. There probably isn't a more upstanding pillar of the community. I do believe I have dined with him at a club in London'.

'Good Lord' Peter replied and went on 'Nevertheless, you cannot deny that Julian appears to have phoned that number'.

'We need to look elsewhere; he definitely would not be involved in any sort of crime'. Reynolds concluded. They parted company.

The next morning Peter kissed the family goodbye and set off to London in his new BMW. He entered the address of the Mercantile and Colonial Bank in to the satellite navigation system and a couple of hours later was in the 'Square Mile'.

Just off Lombard Street he slowed down outside of the Bank. A doorman in uniform stood outside the imposing double oak doors. Peter waited on the yellow lines until a parking space became free. He fed the meter and sat and watched. One or two people went in and out of the building, identifying themselves to the doorman.

At 12.30 precisely a black Rolls Royce Silver Spirit pulled up. Sir John Miles strode out of the building and the doorman opened the rear door of the Rolls. Sir John looked every inch the distinguished banker. Peter took in the details. Dark grey suit, white shirt and Guards tie. The camel coloured overcoat draped around his shoulders. It certainly wasn't cold enough for that, Peter noted. The silver hair worn long and swept back. The face tanned and relaxed. Peter realised that he had only guessed it was him but he was convinced he was right.

The Rolls pulled away and headed for Pall Mall with Peter trailing him. The Rolls stopped outside the Institute of Directors. The driver was out of the car and quickly opened the rear door. Sir John swept in to the building and no doubt lunch was waiting. Peter waited a few moments then entered the building. 'Was that Sir John Miles just gone in?' he said to the Door-man. 'Yes, but you are not a member, sir.'

It's O.K. I'll catch up with him later'. Peter replied.

Peter decided at least he knew what Sir John looked like. He pointed the BMW towards home and drove quickly down the M4.

CHAPTER 49

He was back home before the rest of the family and sat in his study not knowing what to do. He had seen how much money Julian had and how much he was making. Sir John was different, as Chairman of a bank you would expect him to be wealthy. Anyway the Bank no doubt paid for the Rolls and all the trappings of wealth.

On a whim he reached for the phone and called his accountant. Philip, who was Peter's advisor was also the Senior Partner. 'Philip if you thought a business was making huge profits illegally how would you investigate the matter?'

There was a pause while the accountant considered the matter. 'There are industry statistics for every type of business. You know yourself that if your building company is doing well then usually similar businesses are also doing well. Now if you were doing really well in a building recession then that is obviously against the trend'.

Peter said 'How are Bank's doing at the moment?'

Philip replied 'Not very well. They are writing off huge amounts in bad debts following investments in Japan and the third world. But surely you know this. You read the papers'.

'I thought I did but I wanted you to confirm it. If I identified a bank doing really well what is the next step?'

Philip said, 'We would need to study their accounts and look at the share price trend. We also need to research their activities to find out why the profits are higher than expected'.

Peter gave Philip the name of the bank and said 'Start your investigation, I don't care what it costs'.

Philip smiled and thought 'He's never said that before'.

Peter left the study and made a pot of tea in the kitchen. The tea making ritual reminded him of Manuel. He dialled his giant friend and Manuel answered. Peter pictured him in the yard of the farm sat on his old tractor with his shining new phone in his hand. After the usual pleasantries he said 'Could you and Danny get together, use your contacts, and see if a bank called Mercantile and Colonial does any business in Spain. Ask Danny if he has heard Julian speak of them or their Chairman Sir John Miles'.

'I will see what I can do'.

Next he phoned the Police station and asked for someone who could help trace a car. 'Ask C.S. Reynolds if he will authorise a registration number check for me'. There was a delay of 30 seconds.

'Mr Haynes, we have been instructed to give you all assistance, what is the number?'

Peter quoted the number he had committed to memory. The response was 'The car is registered to Sir John Miles' and he gave the address in Holland Park London. Peter jotted it down. He heard the family coming in to the house.

'That's enough for one day'. He decided.

All was quiet for a few days until Philip the accountant rang. 'I think you should come and see me'. When Peter arrived Philip said 'How did you get interested in this?' He gave the accountant a brief resume' of events, leaving out the gory bits. 'You have stumbled onto something strange. Until three years ago Mercantile and Colonial were trading quietly with mediocre profits. In the last few years' profits have rocketed and so has the share price. Coincidentally, that is the time the new Chairman took over so he is doing a good job'.

Peter interjected 'So what is strange?' Philip went on 'There have been no press releases to say they have done any big deals. Usually any business broadcasts good news, it helps to boost the share price'. Peter asked 'What if they were banking huge sums of cash?' Philip replied 'By law they are required to report large deposits of cash or risk being prosecuted under the Money Laundering Act'.

'They would hardly report it, if it was their own cash coming in' Peter responded. 'Tell me Philip, why would a bank this profitable make the Chairman buy his own car?' 'They wouldn't'. 'Next question, Philip, is Sir John Miles a shareholder?'

'Yes a substantial one. That shows faith in his own ability. He bought them the month he joined'.

'If he had sold them recently would you know?'

'Perhaps not, the share register would not necessarily identify him personally. If he were crafty he would sell under a nominee. Director's dealing in their own company shares are always under scrutiny'.

Peter leaned back in his chair 'If he had sold recently would he have made a lot of money?'

'Millions' was the reply.

'Is this insider dealing?'

'Not necessarily. There is no obvious reason for the shares to go up other than the bank is consistently outperforming the market. The shares have not leapt up overnight'.

'Finally Philip, is it sufficiently suspicious to warrant an investigation?'

'Yes I feel it is. If they are clean and honest they have nothing to fear, have they?'

CHAPTER 50

Peter went straight to Supt Reynolds and reported his findings. Supt Reynolds sighed heavily 'You can't expect me to pull him in. He's probably playing golf with the Commissioner this afternoon'.

'Nevertheless, would you do me a favour? Pass this information to the Serious Fraud Office. Keep Sir John's name out of it if you like. Make it a hypothetical case for now'.

'If I refuse?'

'Then I will contact them'.

'That's what I thought'.

Peter returned home and did his best in the home life role. Jane and the boys noticed he had become preoccupied again. But then he usually was.

Philip phoned the next morning 'A large block of shares were sold recently'.

'By whom?'

'It's in the name of a nominee, that's all we know'.

They agreed it was going to be difficult to penetrate that. Bored because nothing was happening Peter phoned Manuel.

'No news for you yet, Peter'.

'Do you think Danny could open the safe at the villa?'

'I will ask him. What are you looking for?'

'I don't know myself, tell me what you find'.

Peter phoned his Manager Ron and said 'Can we go over management accounts tomorrow, please?'

Ron was pleased to have Peter's request but he had not shown much interest in the accounts before. His thinking was 'I will get familiar with reading accounts as fast as I can. My own company ones should be the easiest ones to learn on'.

On the Friday morning Supt Reynolds phoned 'Can you be at the Francis Hotel for 2pm?'

'Yes'.

'Bring your accountant'.

'He may have appointments with clients'.

'Tell him to cancel them or we will fetch him. I want to introduce you to the Serious Fraud Squad'.

Peter and Philip turned up and the others were already there. They were shown to a small meeting room. Peter spoke first 'Why all this cloak and dagger stuff?'

'Two reasons. One, the local nick is not that confidential, I am sorry to say. Two, the SFO men here think you may have a point.'

Peter studied the two men. The younger one spoke 'No we don't look like coppers because we are chartered accountants. Our speciality is Information Technology. Most of the serious crime committed is computer fraud and we expect to have to get in to the bank's files if there is justification'.

Philip gave the two men all the information he had gathered. Peter said 'Are you going to confront Sir John?'

Supt Reynolds took the question 'That is impatient and naïve. You disappoint me, Peter'. He looked at the SFO officers 'Tell them the plan, it's OK'.

'We are going to pose as Inland Revenue Inspectors doing a routine visit. We will not even meet Sir John; his minions will deal with us. We don't expect to uncover anything easily'.

'So what's the point?'

'We will let you know afterwards'. The meeting over, Philip said to all present'

'You know where I am if you want me'.

Chapter 51

Two days later the two SFO men reported to the bank with their briefcases and were taken to the Finance Director's office. The charming man gave them full cooperation and took them to lunch as well. 'You run a very efficient business, Mr Andrews'. 'Thank you, is there anything else you wish to see?'

'Do you have a list of cars the bank owns?'

'Of course, and I assure you that all employees who use a bank car declare it to the taxman'.

'I am sure that is the case'. They looked down the long list of vehicles. 'Can you tell me why the Chairman's Rolls Royce is not listed?'

'Yes, he owns it himself'.

'Why is that, in his position?'

'He refuses to pay the tax liability a car like that would incur. But surely the Inland Revenue does not send two senior inspectors to check on a small matter like this'.

The older inspector spoke, a rare occurrence in itself. 'Mr Andrews, your bank has not been singled out for scrutiny. It is held in high regard and so is Sir John, of course. The Inland Revenue has to be seen to keep an eye on all businesses or else someone will say we show favouritism to a Pillar of the Community. Do you see?'

'Indeed I do' the Finance Director replied.

The small talk continued 'Been with the bank long?'

'About three years'.

Thankfully, at that moment there was a knock on the door and a smartly dressed mature woman entered with tea on a silver tray. She poured the tea and offered biscuits from a bone china platter. As she opened the door to leave, Sir John swept in.

'Good afternoon gentlemen, it's always nice to see the Inland Revenue'.

They smiled dutifully, 'We were just talking about your Rolls Royce. I hear you do not believe in paying tax on company cars'.

'That's it exactly. Come along to my office before you go and have a glass of port'.

They asked the Finance Director a few more questions to make their visit authentic and were then shown along the corridor to Sir John's office. The room also served as the boardroom with a huge mahogany table surrounded by red leather chairs standing on a pale blue Chinese rug. On the table the cut glass decanter caught the sunlight and shone like a diamond. Sir John poured the ruby liquid in to crystal glasses and passed them to the inspectors.

'I don't like my staff to see my personal documents but I want to show you my car purchase detail'.

He produced the car registration document showing him to be the owner. Clipped to it was a sales invoice from one of the London Rolls Royce dealers. The invoice was also in his name. The amount was £65,000. The computer generated invoice also stated "Method of payment-cash".

'You don't need to show us this Sir John, there is no tax liability if you own the car'.

'I have nothing to hide gentleman'.

'Of course not Sir John'. They shook hands and thanked him for his hospitality.

Sir John sat at the head of the table sipping his port. 'That'll teach them to come snooping around. They thought they had me there' he said to himself.

The two men headed straight for the Rolls Royce showroom mentioned on the invoice and asked for the Managing Director. The protective receptionist stated he did not see anyone without an appointment. They produced their warrant cards in unison and the boss was called.

The younger man again did the talking. 'You recall the sale of a Rolls to Sir John Miles?'

'I can't discuss a transaction with you that is confidential'.

'Let me spell it out to you. Sir John paid you all of it in cash and it was agreed that you would issue an invoice for £65,000 and put the rest of the cash in your pocket'. Without a pause he said 'This is the deal, we just want your confirmation that he paid in actual cash. Mention our visit to anyone, particularly Sir John, and we will close you down. We will ensure you go to prison for the shady deals we know you are involved in. We have a file on you'.

The Managing Director, looking rather pale said 'I recall he paid in notes in sealed packets. I will not be contacting him'.

'Remember our arrangement as we will know in minutes if you tip him off'. As soon as they were outside the older officer said 'How did you know he pocketed some of the cash?'

'I didn't, but I checked the market value of the car beforehand and the invoice price was too cheap'.

'What about the file you have on him?'

'I haven't got one.

CHAPTER 52

The next day the two Senior Fraud Officers met with the Registrar of Companies at Companies House. 'We know Sir John Miles bought 800,000 shares at £1-40p each three years ago. We also think he then changed the ownership name on the share certificate to that of a nominee company. Can you tell us how much the shares fetched'? '

'Do you know the name of the nominee company?' asked the registrar.

'No we don't'.

The registrar called in a young chap who looked as though he had yet to start shaving. The problem was explained. The lad sat at the computer and brought Mercantile and Colonial up on the screen.

He retrieved the list of shareholders as of 3 years ago. He clicked the mouse on to Sir John's shareholding. He then suspended this information. Next he swept the records of all transactions up to date. Then he asked the computer to home in on all transactions involving 500,000 to one million shares.

By selective retrieval he produced the number of shares in this category that were sold by nominees. Next he retrieved the original shareholding and introduced it to the nominee sale. He pressed the print button and tore off the sheet. It showed original purchase name, number of shares and price paid. It also showed sale price date and Nominee Company with a Liechenstein address. The profit on the transaction was £2.4 million.

The investigators took the printout and returned to Bath for a meeting with Supt Reynolds and Peter the following day. They explained their findings. 'The problem is he has done nothing illegal. Unless he attempts to bring that money in to this country he is not liable for tax.

Peter spoke 'I wonder if the money is still in Liechenstein'.

Supt Reynolds commented 'All we have so far is Julian may have phoned him. He made a killing on the stock market and he bought a Rolls for cash. This man is untouchable'.

Peter asked 'I wonder where his original cash came from?'

One of the investigators said 'From our experience you would have to trace his career and earnings over a period of years. We can get the authority to see the bank statements of anyone under suspicion.

The trouble in this case is, if we get that authority, it will be to see his accounts at his bank. In other words we will tip him off immediately. He will have the best legal advice available and we have nothing other than a questionable phone call. Come to think of it he might say that his telephone number is not issued to anyone so this Julian misdialled by accident. Can you imagine the libel action?'

CHAPTER 53

Peter went home seemingly blocked at every turn. He phoned Manuel 'Did Danny get in to the safe at the villa?'

'Yes he did but it wasn't difficult the door was already open. We think when Julian left with the money he took all the documents as well. It was completely empty'.

Manuel's slow deliberate English emphasised the disappointment. Another blank.

Supt Reynolds phoned 'I am sorry Peter I cannot devote any more time to this without something more definite'.

Peter replied 'Do you mind if I continue to snoop around?'

'No but don't pose as a Police Officer'. Peter smiled at the reference to his previous methods.

That night he lay in bed and wondered if it was all worth it. He had the revenge he wanted. 'I don't know how to give up, that's my trouble'. He slipped out of bed and began packing a few clothes. He phoned reservations at Heathrow 'Can I get a night flight to Zurich?'

'Yes you can, we fly to Zurich every few hours'.

He left a note for Jane and slipped out of the house. Less than 2 hours later he was in the departure lounge. He had not finished his second coffee when his flight was called. Landing in Zurich he picked up a hire car and headed for Liechenstein. It was nearly lunchtime when he drove into the Principality.

He found the Police station and told them what he wanted. He asked that they phone Supt Reynolds, on the number he gave them, for authorisation.

'We can't give you a list of nominee companies based in Liechenstein'.

'If I gave you the company name would you tell me the address where it is registered?'

'Yes, but I don't see how you would obtain it'.

Peter gave them the printout to look at. He was given the address.

Driving down the street all he could see was closed doors with little brass plates. Not all the plates had company names on them, just numbers. But he had written the number of the office address on the printout. He located the door and parked the car where he could observe.

It was a reasonable guess that they would close the office about 4.30 p.m. Once again he played the waiting game. As predicted, late afternoon about 12 people came out. Peter got out of his car and leaned against it. Three young girls walked off together and the others went their separate ways.

He followed the girls in to a little tea shop. Once they were settled he approached their table and said apologetically 'Could you please help me to order tea. I have trouble with your language'. He was soon chatting to them.

One of the girls with flaxen hair and bright blue eyes said 'I have a brother in London'. Soon the conversation was between her and Peter. The other girls left them together and said their goodbyes.

'My name is Gertrude and I did not want to say this in front of my friends but my brother is a drug addict. He is very much alone and my parents forbid me to try to visit him. I know I have only just met you but if I gave you the hostel address in London would you consider visiting him?'

Peter spoke. 'Before I ask you something, you have my word that I will do as you ask. You and I will discuss how I can help him. Now, that deal is done, as we say. I am an investigator gathering information on a drug dealer in London. This man is the mastermind behind the acquisition and distribution. He uses a nominee company to move money around. That nominee company is administered by your office'.

Gertrude had listened intently and her blue eyes grew wider. She said nothing and this made Peter worry before he asked the favour. So he put it to her carefully.

'You could lose your job for this. So the choice is yours. Could you open the files of the company whose name I will give you? Before you answer, remember, I will help your brother anyway, but this company is a front for drug dealing'.

Gertrude spoke 'I will help you'.

Peter went on 'When you retrieve the information ensure you cannot be traced. I am looking for interaction between the nominee, Mercantile and Colonial Bank,

Sir John Mills and a Spanish bank hopefully with a customer named Julian Wilding, but I expect it will be just a numbered account'.

Gertrude stood up 'Meet me here tomorrow, same time, and I will have the information'.

CHAPTER 54

Peter booked in to a nearby hotel and had a leisurely dinner. The menu was printed in several languages. He read it thoroughly and noted the emphasis on heavy carbohydrate food like dumplings. 'Must be to keep up the energy, for skiers'.

In the morning he walked around the tiny principality, phoned home and generally whiled away the time. In the afternoon he made for the tea shop and Gertrude was punctual. She handed him a laser printed sheet and he quickly read the transaction detail. He stood up and walked around the table. He gave her a quick hug, kissed her on the cheek and returned to his seat blushing.

'Give me a note of your brother's address. I won't give him money but I will get him in to a rehabilitation centre. I will also get him re-established in work when he is well or arrange for him to return to you'.

Gertrude said 'But I could never pay for all that'.

'Join me for dinner tonight, instead'.

'And afterwards?'

'I am much older than you' he replied.

'Yes but you look fit enough'.

He studied her for a few seconds. 'See you at this hotel about 7.30 p.m'. He gave her the hotel brochure.

The next morning he showered and dressed and brought the coffee over to the bed. The blond hair spread across the pillow and the sturdy shoulders visible above the duvet. He stroked her cheek and she gradually opened her eyes.

'You know I must leave now. Don't be late for work and thank you for the business and the pleasure'.

'Thank you, kind sir, it was an education'.

As he drove to the airport he pondered on his infidelity. 'It's all in the line of duty. Anyway, men are different. Women need a reason. Men just need a place'. Within 3 hours he was driving down the M4.

Jane was so pleased to see him, he felt guilty. He gave Sue the evening off and opened a bottle of wine. Jane giggled as he tried to get her to drink through a straw.

The following day he went in to Bath and headed for the library. He photocopied the information Gertrude had obtained and walked up to Queens Square to his solicitors.

He asked the receptionist for an envelope and put the copy inside. He sealed it and wrote his name on it and also that of Superintendent Reynolds. 'Put that in the strong room please'.

The receptionist said 'Don't you want to speak to your solicitor?'

'I can't afford it'.

'I knew you would say that'.

That evening he said 'Jane do you mind if I go and walk around Bath?' This was something he frequently did and drove the car down Pulteney Street to the roundabout and turned in to Henrietta Street. There were no parking spaces until he was halfway down and stopped outside the park.

Walking back he passed the garden known locally as the 'Blind Garden'. Correctly, it is a garden dedicated to the blind with flowers and shrubs selected for their scent. His mind wandered back to the exotic bougainvillaea of Spain. So far he had been unable to decide how to use Gertrude's information, afraid that Sir John's heavyweight lawyers would still beat anything Supt Reynolds could present.

Without realising it he came to Julian's flat. He had forgotten about this as the route was his familiar 'constitutional walk' when he wanted time to himself. There was a light on! His heart pounded and a shiver went up his spine. 'He was dead all right, then Danny set fire to him, and then drowned him. That would be enough for most people'. Peter had no regrets and his callous recollection made him smile. He walked through the arch and in to the mews. 'It will be interesting to see if there's a car in the garage'.

He looked at the door lock and took out his credit card from his wallet. Sliding the card in to the old Yale lock he stepped inside. Walking to the front of the big dark coloured car there was no mistaking the Rolls Royce Silver Spirit grille. He recognised the registration number; it belonged to Sir John Miles. He left quietly and returned to his car. Parking spaces were appearing as people left the restaurants in Argyle Street. He moved the car a bit nearer to the flat. Once again he settled down to wait.

Daylight came and still no one appeared. At 9.30 a.m. a parking warden tapped on the window and made him jump. 'It's a two hour limit sir'.

'I am on surveillance but have no I.D. for security reasons'. The warden said 'I think I've heard them all now' and walked on.

Sir John emerged from the front door in expensive casual clothes. Holding his hands were a girl and a boy about 10 years old. They walked down the path and in to the park. Peter followed at a safe distance. Sir John produced a 'Frisbee' and watched the children spinning it to each other. Saying something Peter could not hear he headed back to the flat.

Thinking quickly, Peter sprinted to an ice cream van parked in the road. He bought two ninety nines and approached the children.

'I was asked to bring you these'. They took them readily. Peter did his best to befriend them. Their eyes shone brightly, but he noticed how thin they were. Black rings surrounded those huge eyes. Finishing their ice creams they carried on with their game. They both took off their tracksuit tops as they became hot.

The little T shirts exposed their skinny arms. The tell tale little marks on the inside of their arms confirmed his worst fears. He slipped quietly away. In the car he phoned the Police station and asked them to find out if Sir John had a wife and family. A few minutes later his mobile rang. 'He's a bachelor'. Peter returned home.

He went to Josh's bedroom and picked up his camera. 'I hope he won't mind'. He made a couple of phone calls. One was to track down P C Enfield. 'I am in a position to give your career a boost. Can you meet me at the arch in Henrietta Street at 10.30 tonight? Also can you bring a solicitor of your choice? I suggest Supt Reynolds' favourite one'.

P C Enfield replied 'I will do it but don't put me in a difficult position'. 'It's not you I have in mind'. Peter laughed at his own private joke. He made one more phone call to a dubious character he would deny knowing if asked.

CHAPTER 55

At 10.15p.m. precisely, Peter and his small time burglar approached the outer front door of the house. In seconds they were inside. Peter listened at the door and nodded. The burglar tried several skeleton keys until one silently turned the dead lock. They went back to the outer door.

Peter put four fifty pound notes in the burglar's hand. Not a word was spoken and his accomplice walked off. Peter kept the door open with his foot and his camera in his hand. P C Enfield arrived with the solicitor, James Francis.

Very briefly he told them what to expect. P C Enfield gently opened the door and crept through the hall to the bedroom. He pushed open the door. Peter was through and taking pictures as fast as he could. Sir John was naked on the bed. The children also naked were performing acts that the three would never forget. The solicitor looked sickened.

P C Enfield was all for handcuffing Sir John. Peter had guessed what they would find and had prepared himself, although the depravity was worse than he thought it would be. 'Don't handcuff him, he would probably enjoy that as well, just hold him there'. He tried to defuse the situation.

James Francis recovered 'Phone for a Policewoman and Social Services'.

Peter found the syringe and drugs on the bedside table for all to see. He photographed them making sure Sir John was also in the photos as he still lay on the bed. They ushered the children out of the bedroom hoping Social Services would come quickly.

Sir John had not spoken but was sweating profusely. Peter would not allow him to cover up. He introduced the other two but omitted his own identity so that Sir John would assume he was a Police Officer.

'Now, Sir John, we have you on suspicion of fraud, and read out details from the Liechenstein print out. You have among other things, defrauded the bank. Even though you put the money in to the bank's account you took it out without authority. We will, of course, want to know where the money came from. You are directly involved in drug trafficking with Julian Wilding. Finally, you sir, are a child molester and supplying drugs to minors as well'.

Surprisingly, Sir John spoke in a level voice. 'With my reputation, the best lawyers money can…'.

Peter cut in. 'We are here to do a deal. As you well know we had Officers killed in the Fulham explosion. It is the people responsible for that we are after. Those Coppers all had families. If we have you for fraud, or tax evasion if you wish, you may not even go to prison. Whereas if you serve time for drug trafficking and involving children in the kind of games we have seen tonight, life will be hell on earth for you in prison.'

'When I smuggle these photographs in to the prison you will be raped every night. Believe me you won't like that as much as you think.' The other two smiled briefly. Sir John hardly hesitated; he listed off from memory the names of the key men present in the warehouse that night. He also implicated the Finance Director and Head of Security at the Bank. P C Enfield and James Francis listened and wrote as fast as they could. Peter already knew the story.

P C Enfield was desperately trying to convey the reminder to Peter that he was not a Police Officer without actually saying so. He said. 'I am arresting you for conspiracy to defraud'.

'OK' said Sir John.

Peter spoke 'And?'

'And drug trafficking, child molestation and administering drugs to children'.

'But you said, just fraud'. Sir John, still naked, leapt off the bed, shouting and trying to rain blows on Peter. Peter just stuck his straight fingers in to the ample stomach of Sir John's large body and he doubled up gasping.

'You said, just fraud, nothing else' he groaned.

'I lied' Peter replied handing the camera to PC Enfield.

Sir John, still not beaten said 'You, a Police Officer, admits to lying in front of a solicitor. You have blown it, you pathetic little man'.

Peter was ready with his reply 'I am not a Police Officer and I did not say I was. The tape recorder will confirm that'.

James Francis was having trouble switching off the tape recorder he had concealed, but it had done its job. He apologised 'I am not terribly au fait with these contraptions'.

Peter spoke for the last time. 'P C Enfield you had better put the cuffs on him now and lead him out. Can I have the camera back a minute'?

P C Enfield said 'Better get him some clothes'. 'No they'll give him a blanket at the station'. Peter walked out first. Sir John, with hands cuffed, walked stark naked, towards Peter, who stood on the other side of the road. Peter unrolled a little poster he had brought and gave it to Sir John to hold in front of him. He clicked the camera and caught Sir John full frontal. 'I will make sure Supt Reynolds gets a copy of the photo but the priority is to catch tonight's edition of the Bath Chronicle'. The caption read 'Pillar of the Community'.

Peter walked off in to the night.

ISBN 141202649-0